Anna & Elsa

#1: All Hail the Queen

#2: Memory and Magic

By Erica David

Illustrated by Bill Robinson
and Manuela Razzi

Random House  New York

For Ken & Judy David —E.D.

DISNEP

Anna & Elsa

#1: All Hail the Queen
#2: Memory and Magic

rhcbooks.com

ISBN 978-0-7364-4000-4

Printed in the United States of America

10 9 8 7 6 5 4 3 2 1

DISNEY
Anna & Elsa

#1: All Hail the Queen

By Erica David

Illustrated by Bill Robinson
and Manuela Razzi

Random House  New York

Chapter 1

Queen Elsa of Arendelle looked out one of her castle windows. It was a glorious morning in the kingdom. The sun shone brightly. It danced across the waters of the fjord.

Below, the people of Arendelle were just starting the day. Shopkeepers opened their windows and doors. Fishermen walked to the wharf. Ice harvesters set out for the frozen lake nestled in the mountains.

Elsa was proud of her village and the people in it. They had come to trust her, even though she wasn't like most queens. Most queens couldn't cast spells of ice and snow. Most queens couldn't make a walking, talking snowman. Most queens couldn't accidentally set off an eternal winter, leaving the village completely frozen! Not so long ago, Elsa had been worried that the people of Arendelle wouldn't accept her because of her differences, but to her delight, they had embraced her wholeheartedly.

Elsa stepped back from the window.

The beautiful weather made her long to go outdoors, but she had royal duties to attend to. She turned to her desk. The plans she had been working on for the town's new plumbing system were waiting. The pipes and canals would carry water to every part of the village. But the builders couldn't start without the queen's go-ahead.

Elsa sat down and picked up the plans. Seconds later, the door to her study sprang open. Her younger sister, Anna, bounded into the room. Her eyes were brimming with excitement.

"Do you know what day it is?" Anna asked eagerly.

"Tuesday?" Elsa guessed.

"Today's the day we cross number three off the list!" Anna exclaimed. She hurried over to her sister, unrolling a long scroll of paper. It was Anna's list of Things to Do in Arendelle. She'd been keeping it ever since Elsa became queen. Anna cleared her throat to announce number three.

"Florian's Famous Flangendorfers!" she said.

"Flangen—what?" Elsa asked.

"Flangendorfers. The most delicious dessert in all of Arendelle," Anna explained cheerfully.

Elsa shook her head, puzzled. She'd never heard of a flangendorfer.

"Aren't you excited?" Anna asked. She took Elsa's hand and pulled her to her feet.

"I am, but I have work to do," Elsa replied.

"How can you work on a day like this?" Anna said. She twirled around in the shaft of sunlight shining through the windows. "Come on, Elsa, just one flangendorfer."

Elsa bit her lip as she considered. It was such a beautiful day. One flangendorfer wouldn't hurt. "Okay," she agreed.

Anna whooped with delight. "I love our visits to the village," she said. "There's a whole world out there!"

Anna's excitement was contagious. Elsa couldn't help smiling.

The sisters walked through the palace gates. They strolled along the cobblestone streets of the town.

By now the village shops had opened. The town square was filled with merchants. Some wheeled carts of fruit for sale. Others sold beautiful scarves and jewelry. Many waved to Anna and Elsa.

"Isn't this wonderful?" Anna said. "Just look at all there is to see!"

Elsa noticed a small girl making her way through the crowd. The girl carried a bouquet of fresh flowers. She had two dark braids that bobbed up and down. She skipped happily toward Elsa and Anna.

The little girl held her flowers up to Elsa. Elsa smiled and reached out to take the bouquet. "What's your name?" she asked gently.

"Ingrid," the girl said quietly. Now

that she was face to face with the queen, she seemed nervous. Ingrid lowered her eyes and dropped into a deep curtsy.

"It's okay. Don't be shy," Elsa said. She took the bouquet from the girl's trembling fingers. "Thank you for the flowers."

Ingrid remained absolutely still. She looked like she had no idea what to do.

Anna noticed the girl's confusion and gently raised her from her curtsy. She leaned down to whisper in Ingrid's ear. "She's not as intimidating as she looks," Anna joked, pointing to her sister, who was smiling. Elsa didn't look the least bit intimidating.

Ingrid giggled. She waved timidly to the queen. Elsa waved back.

"Oh, what's that on your dress?" Anna asked Ingrid. She pointed to the child's bright blue pinafore.

Curious, Ingrid glanced down. As soon as she did, Anna playfully tweaked her nose. "Just kidding," she said.

Ingrid laughed and squealed in delight. She seemed to forget her nervousness about meeting the queen. She made another curtsy and darted off into the square.

"How adorable," Anna said, leaning over to sniff the flowers. She plucked a sprig of purple heather from Elsa's bouquet and tucked it behind her ear. Elsa smiled. Anna definitely had a way with people.

The sisters weaved through the crowd of villagers in the square.

"Are you sure you know where you're going?" Elsa asked.

"Of course!" Anna replied. "I've been planning this visit forever!"

"Forever?" Elsa said doubtfully.

"Well, maybe not *forever*," Anna admitted. "But at least since you became queen."

Elsa remembered the day of her coronation. Until then, the castle gates had been shut. None of the villagers had been allowed inside. It was all because Elsa hadn't wanted her powers to hurt anyone. She had thought the only way to keep everyone safe had been to keep them out.

On the day she became queen, though,

the castle gates had been opened wide. Back then, Elsa had been worried about her secret. She had been nervous about meeting the townspeople. Anna, on the other hand, couldn't wait to welcome them.

Now Elsa was relieved that she didn't have to hide her powers anymore. She and Anna could leave the palace any time they liked. But although Elsa was free to explore, new people and places took some getting used to after all those years alone.

Lost in thought, Elsa didn't notice the gruff fisherman in front of her. She accidentally walked into him, knocking his basket of fish onto the cobblestones.

"I'm so sorry," Elsa said.

The fisherman grumbled until he

realized who she was. One look at Elsa and his entire expression changed. "No, I'm sorry, Your Majesty," he said formally.

"Please, it was my fault," Elsa said, smiling. She bent down to gather up the fish.

"No, no! I'll take care of that," the fisherman insisted. He bowed deeply and waved the queen aside.

Elsa hesitated. She didn't want the villagers to treat her differently just because she was the queen. She wanted to help.

Anna had been watching the whole scene. She tapped the fisherman on the shoulder.

"Hey, she's not that kind of queen,"

Anna whispered conspiratorially.

"What kind of queen is that?" the
fisherman asked.

"The off-with-his-head kind," Anna
replied. "She's the kind who really wants
to pick up the fish. I think you should let
her do it."

The fisherman looked from Anna to Elsa and back to Anna again. "Are you sure?" he said.

"I'm sure. In fact, the *princess* insists," Anna said, pointing to herself.

The fisherman relaxed. A broad smile spread across his face. "Well, if the *princess* insists," he said. He moved aside and let Elsa help him collect his fish. In no time, they'd placed all of the shiny silver trout in the basket.

The fisherman thanked Elsa and Anna for their help. He disappeared into the crowd with his fish.

"How do you do that?" Elsa asked.

"Do what?" Anna said.

"He was worried I'd be angry, but you

knew just what to say," Elsa explained.

"I don't know," Anna said, shrugging. "It's not magic. I just talked to him. I guess I'm a talker."

"I talked to him, too," Elsa pointed out.

"Yes, but you're very . . . queenly," Anna said, grinning. She held up her hand and waved stiffly to the crowd to demonstrate.

"I don't wave like that," Elsa said, laughing. "You make me look like some kind of ice princess."

"Well, aren't you?" Anna teased gently.

"I prefer snow queen," Elsa said lightheartedly. "*You're* the princess."

Anna laughed. The sisters linked arms and crossed the square.

"We're almost there," Anna said.

Florian's Famous Flangendorfers was just down the road. Elsa could already smell the sweet pastries.

Just then, her ears pricked up. A band of village musicians was playing at the edge of the square. The townspeople had gathered to listen. They clapped and swayed to the music.

Elsa and Anna were charmed by the bubbly melody. They walked closer to the band, clapping and snapping along. Elsa drew several coins from her purse. She dropped them into a nearby jar for the musicians.

The musicians recognized Elsa at once. They stopped playing and bowed deeply to the queen. Then they picked up their instruments again. They played a slow, dignified song. It was Arendelle's royal anthem.

Elsa tried her best to clap along, but the song was too slow. It sounded nothing like the cheerful song the band had been playing moments before. The villagers began to fidget. Arendelle's royal anthem wasn't just slow—it was also long.

Suddenly, Anna hitched up her skirts. She kicked up her heels and started to dance. The musicians noticed and played faster. They wanted to keep up with Anna's sprightly steps. Elsa laughed and danced along with Anna. The anthem had never sounded so good!

Soon the villagers joined the dancing

queen and her sister. Everyone moved happily in time to the music. Elsa and Anna danced across the cobblestones all the way to Florian's Famous Flangendorfers.

Chapter 2

Florian's Famous Flangendorfers was more than just a bakery—it was a dessert lover's dream. From the outside, it looked like a gingerbread house. The roof seemed to be made of gumdrops. The front door was painted in a red-and-white peppermint swirl. Elsa had never seen anything like it.

The shop itself looked good enough to eat.

Inside, the bakery was bright and airy. Beautiful glass display cabinets lined the walls. One cabinet was full of gooey toffees and sticky taffies. Another displayed row after row of chocolate bonbons.

Florian's candies looked delicious, but he was really known for his pastries. The buttery croissants, creamy cream puffs, sugary krumkake, and heavenly cakes were kept on the bakery counter at the rear of the shop.

Elsa and Anna drifted toward the counter. They were pulled in by the mouthwatering scent of freshly baked pies.

"Ahem!" said a voice. Elsa and Anna looked up from the pastries. A tall, thin man stood before them. He had a long, narrow face and wore a crisp white chef's coat. A black beret sat on top of his head.

The man swept forward to greet them. "My queen, allow me to introduce myself," he said. "Chef Florian, at your service."

Chef Florian bowed and kissed the back of Elsa's hand. She jumped in surprise. Elsa hadn't expected Florian's dramatic manner. She gave Anna a look that said *This flangendorfer better be good.* Anna smiled sheepishly. She shook hands with Chef Florian but pulled away before he could kiss her hand, too.

Chef Florian didn't seem to notice. He simply snapped his fingers. At the sound, two assistant bakers came from the back of the shop. They carried a fancy table and two chairs. The bakers set the table and chairs down between Anna and Elsa.

"Please, sit," Florian said. He snapped again and another assistant appeared. She held a large platter covered with a shiny silver dome.

Elsa glanced at the huge dome. Her eyes caught Anna's across the table. She leaned forward and whispered, "Anna, what's a flangendorfer again?"

Anna shrugged. "I don't know," she whispered back. "But I hear they're delicious!"

Elsa hoped her sister was right. From the size of the platter, it looked like they had a lot of flangendorfer ahead of them.

"May I present to you the finest dessert in all of Arendelle!" Chef Florian exclaimed. He removed the silver dome with a flourish.

On the platter sat two towering pastries. Each flangendorfer was made of five layers stacked on top of each other. The bottom and top layers were light, flaky pastry. The middle layers were made of fruit, chocolate, and cream. The whole dessert was drizzled with honey. Then it was dusted with powdered sugar.

Elsa gasped, amazed. She picked up her spoon. One bite was all it took to convince her. *Chef Florian is a genius!* Elsa could tell that Anna had the same thought. Here

was everything she loved, all in one dessert!

The bakery grew quiet. The only sound was the clattering of spoons against plates. When the sisters finished eating, they relaxed in their seats. Their bellies were quite full. They smiled contentedly.

"Who wants seconds?" Chef Florian asked.

"That was wonderful," Elsa said. "But I don't think I could eat another bite."

Anna opened her mouth to agree. But it wasn't words that came out. Instead, she gave a long, loud belch.

Chef Florian was stunned. He clearly hadn't been expecting that—especially from a princess.

"Anna!" Elsa said, embarrassed.

Anna shrugged apologetically. "Excuse me," she said.

Then Florian began to chuckle. It started quietly at first. But the sound grew until it was a full-fledged laugh.

"That's the best compliment a chef can

get," he said to Anna. "Come, I'll show you the secrets of the flangendorfer."

*

Florian led Elsa and Anna through a curtain behind the bakery counter. On the other side was an enormous kitchen. The kitchen was a blur of activity. Florian's assistants ran back and forth in a swirl of flour dust. They rolled dough, melted chocolate, and piped icing onto delicious treats.

"My family has been making flangendorfers for years," Florian said proudly. "The dessert was invented by my great-great-great-great-great-uncle a long time ago."

"How did he come up with it?" Elsa asked.

"An excellent question!" Florian said. "But the answer is a mystery. Some say he got the recipe from the trolls."

Elsa remembered the trolls. They knew a great deal of magic. But she'd never thought of them as pastry people.

"I think he just put all the best sweet stuff together and—*bam!*—flangendorfer!" Anna said.

"I wouldn't be surprised," Florian replied. "Great-Uncle Klaus loved to eat."

The pastry chef took the sisters over to a nearby table. In the middle was a large mound of dough. Florian divided the dough in half, giving one part to Elsa and the other to Anna.

"This is our special flangendorfer dough," he explained. "I will teach you how to roll it flat."

Anna pushed up her sleeves confidently. She'd baked cookies in the palace kitchens. "Piece of cake," she said breezily.

Florian shot her a warning look. When it came to baking, he was all business.

"Er, flangendorfer, I meant. Piece of flangendorfer," Anna said seriously. She stood up straight.

Florian turned his attention to the dough. "First you must remember to be very quiet," he whispered.

"Quiet? Why?" Anna blurted out.

"Shhhhh!" Florian hissed. "The dough, she is very sensitive."

"She?" Elsa asked. Anna looked at her sister and smothered a giggle.

"Yes. She. The dough is like a fiery princess. You must not make her angry," he explained. "You must speak gently to her . . . with your fingers."

Florian wiggled his flour-covered fingers in the air. He curled one hand into a fist and punched the dough flat.

"That doesn't look very gentle," Anna whispered to Elsa. Elsa did her best not to laugh, but Anna was making it difficult.

Instead, Elsa focused on Florian's instructions. She punched her dough and pressed it flat with her fingertips. The finicky pastry chef inspected her work.

When he was satisfied, he handed her a rolling pin.

Anna's dough was giving her trouble. It stuck to her fingers in a gluey ball. Luckily, Florian didn't notice. He stepped away to check on a batch of cream puffs.

"I think she's angry with me," Anna said softly.

"Who?" Elsa whispered.

"The fiery princess dough!" Anna replied. "She's stuck to my fingers!" Anna shook her hands desperately. But the dough didn't budge.

"Maybe you should apologize to her," Elsa teased.

"What?" Anna laughed.

"Shhhhh!" Elsa replied. "You heard

Chef Florian. He told us to whisper."

Anna sighed in frustration. She wiped one sticky hand against the front of her dress, but that only made things worse. "Now *I'm* stuck!" she whispered to Elsa, trying to tug her hand away from the dough.

Elsa calmly scooped some extra flour into her hands. She sprinkled the flour onto Anna's dough, hoping to make it less sticky.

Unfortunately, the flour tickled Anna's nose. *"ACHOO!"* A gust of flour dust rose into the air when she sneezed. It settled in her hair and on her eyelashes like a fine coating of snow.

Anna reached for a towel to wipe her

face but accidentally backed into a shelf of pots. The shelf toppled, sending pots and pans clattering to the ground with a loud *crash*!

One pot fell into a giant bowl of batter being mixed by an assistant. A big blob splashed out of the bowl, sailed across the kitchen, and landed right on top of the lantern. The flame went out.

Chef Florian peered angrily through the dark. He spotted Anna at the center of the commotion. Anna grinned guiltily. In the silence that followed, she nervously licked the dough from her fingers.

Florian huffed and folded his arms across his chest. Anna tried to open her mouth to apologize, but again no words came out. "Mmmph!" Anna mumbled urgently. "MMMPH!"

All the chefs and assistants stared at Anna, dumbfounded. Then Elsa realized— Anna had eaten so much dough, her lips were stuck together!

*

That night, Anna was sitting on the end of Elsa's bed in her pajamas. Her list of Things to Do in Arendelle was spread out on her lap. "I can't wait for number four tomorrow!" she exclaimed.

"Wasn't number three enough?" Elsa asked wearily.

"So I made a little mess in Chef Florian's kitchen," Anna said with a shrug.

"Everything turned out okay in the end."

Elsa laughed. Her sister was right. Somehow everything *had* turned out okay. Even though Anna had brought the whole kitchen to a halt, Chef Florian couldn't stay angry at her. He had laughed so hard that she was immediately back in his good graces. It was true. Anna definitely had a way with people.

It was something Elsa admired about her sister. Elsa wondered if she would ever have that kind of relationship with her subjects—without the mess, she hoped!

Chapter 3

The next afternoon, three visitors arrived in the palace courtyard. They were an unusual trio. First there was Sven, a shaggy, playful reindeer. Then there was Kristoff, an ice harvester who had been raised by trolls. Finally, there was Olaf.

Olaf was a snowman who loved

sunshine and warm hugs. Also, Olaf could talk! In fact, he was talking right now. "I can't wait to get to the lake!" he said. Olaf waved his tiny twig arms in delight.

"Slow down, there," said Kristoff. "We can't leave without Anna and Elsa." Kristoff had promised everyone a tour of the frozen lake high in the mountains. It was number four on Anna's adventure list.

"We're here!" Elsa called. She and Anna walked into the courtyard. They waved happily to Kristoff, Olaf, and Sven. Sven snorted contentedly in his bridle, pulling Kristoff and Olaf in the cart closer to the sisters.

Anna patted Sven's muzzle. The

reindeer nuzzled her gently until he found what he was looking for. In the pocket of Anna's dress was a big, juicy carrot. Sven chomped the carrot with pleasure. Carrots were his favorite treat.

Next it was Elsa's turn to greet the reindeer. She scratched him softly between the antlers. Sven nosed through her pockets but was ultimately disappointed. The queen's pockets were empty! The reindeer snorted his disapproval.

"Hey, not everyone has to bring you carrots, buddy," Kristoff said from his perch in the front of the cart.

Sven turned away from him with his nose in the air.

"Don't mind him," Kristoff said to

Elsa. "Somebody woke up on the wrong side of the barn this morning."

"I didn't!" Olaf offered helpfully.

"I know. I was talking about Mr. Cranky Caribou," Kristoff replied, pointing to Sven.

"Mr. Caribou?" Olaf asked, confused. "I don't think I've met him."

"Of course you've met him!" Kristoff said.

"It's okay, Olaf," Anna interrupted. "You'll meet him someday." She liked to play along with Olaf.

Kristoff jumped down and helped Elsa and Anna into the cart. Then he took his place in the driver's seat. Moments later, they were on their way.

The journey to the frozen lake was a

familiar one for Sven. He and Kristoff had been going there since they were little. They had worked side by side with the ice harvesters for a long time.

Sven climbed higher and higher until they reached the lake. It was surrounded by snow-capped mountains. The frozen water glowed a bright shade of pale blue. A group of hardy men and women worked on the icy surface.

"This is where the magic happens," Kristoff said proudly. He introduced Elsa, Anna, and Olaf to his fellow ice harvesters. The workers were honored to meet the queen, the princess, and the snowman. They bowed deeply and welcomed them.

"Everyone here works together,"

Kristoff explained. The ice harvesters split up into small groups. The first group cut the frozen surface with long saws. They carved blocks of ice from the lake.

Elsa watched, fascinated. The ice harvesters were part of Arendelle's history. They'd been supplying the village with ice for hundreds of years!

Anna saw the rapt expression on her sister's face. "Not bad for number four on the list," Anna whispered to her. Elsa smiled in return. She was thrilled.

Together, they followed Kristoff over to the next group of workers. The men stood over the newly cut block of ice. The ice blocks bobbed up and down on the freezing surface. The harvesters used sturdy tongs to bring the blocks out of the water.

"Can I try?" Anna asked.

"I don't know. The ice is very heavy," Kristoff said dramatically. "Allow me."

Kristoff flexed his muscles, showing off. He fixed his tongs to a block of ice. "Now, what I'm about to do here requires years of training," he said. "Oh, and it doesn't hurt to be strong and robust."

Elsa and Anna rolled their eyes. They knew Kristoff was trying to impress them.

Kristoff lifted the tongs and placed them on the ice block. He heaved his weight toward the block. It bobbed in the water but didn't pop out like it was supposed to. Kristoff laughed nervously and glanced at the sisters.

"I don't think that's how it's supposed to work," Elsa whispered to Anna. Anna laughed.

After several more failed tries, Kristoff finally got the ice block to bob awkwardly out of the water and onto the frozen surface. "And that is how we harvest ice," he said.

Anna took the tongs from Kristoff and walked over to the next block of ice. She easily bobbed it down, so that it popped up and slid onto the surface beside Olaf.

Kristoff's mouth dropped open in surprise. "No way," he said.

"Maybe you should practice more," Elsa told him. She patted Anna on the back.

Olaf stared at the large cube of ice

beside him. It seemed to sparkle with a light all its own. The ice block was almost as big as he was.

"Hey, we have a lot in common, don't we?" Olaf asked the ice. "I'm handsome, you're handsome. I like warm hugs, you like warm hugs. . . . It's like we're family."

Before Elsa knew it, Olaf was pushing the block of ice toward her.

"Elsa! Elsa, look!" he cried excitedly. "It's my cousin!"

Elsa smiled at Olaf. It was sweet, the way he liked every creature he met—even a block of ice that couldn't move. For a moment, Elsa wondered whether she might be able to bring the ice block to life as a real cousin for Olaf. But she didn't need to. Olaf already loved his ice-block cousin just the way it was.

"Cousins are great, aren't they? They're just like . . . like sisters," said Olaf, gazing at Anna.

"Sisters are great, Olaf, and so are cousins," Anna said, "but you have another family, too."

"Oh. I do?" Olaf asked, puzzled.

"You do," Elsa answered. "You have us."

"Oh, yeah!" Olaf said. Now he seemed even happier.

Olaf scrambled to keep up with Kristoff, leaving the ice block behind. The mountain man led them to the final group of harvesters.

"Once the ice comes out of the lake, we load it onto sleds," Kristoff explained. "Then we take the ice into town to sell it."

Elsa watched the harvesters carry ice blocks on their shoulders. They brought them to the sleds waiting on the ice and carefully loaded each one. Everyone worked together, just as Kristoff had said.

"Seeing these blocks together gives me a happy feeling!" Olaf declared. "They're a family, just like us. They even get to ride to town together!"

Olaf looked over his shoulder to see the block of ice he'd left behind. It was all alone. "We forgot one!" he cried. "He has to go to town with his family!"

Elsa watched Olaf race back to the lonely ice block. He pushed it across the frozen lake to the sleds piled high with ice. Olaf tried to lift the block, but his twig arms weren't strong enough!

Elsa hurried over to help the snowman. They each took one side and started to lift. Elsa could move the block a little, but Olaf's side stayed firmly on the lake's surface. The big block slid around as they tried to lift it. Then Anna and Kristoff joined them, and each lifted a corner. At last, with everyone's help, the ice block was settled onto the sled. Olaf waved his twig arms in victory.

Just then, the frozen lake beneath the sled creaked loudly. Large cracks split the surface under the runners. With the extra block of ice, the sled was too heavy!

"Quick, run!" Kristoff yelled.

Everyone hurried away from the sleds. They reached the banks of the lake just in time. The cracks in the ice widened and a huge hole appeared. Three sleds sank into the water, leaving the ice blocks floating on the surface.

Chapter 4

The ice harvesters were a tall, burly group of men and women. They were known for their strength. They were also known for singing songs while they worked. For the most part, they were pleasant people. But they didn't look so pleasant now.

"Olaf was only trying to help," Anna said. "We all were."

The ice harvesters grumbled. Their mouths were turned down into frowns.

"Don't worry, I can fix it!" Olaf said happily. "I'm an ice man, too."

"Technically, you're a *snow*man," Anna pointed out.

Elsa thought about the fisherman she'd met the day before. She'd been so happy when he had let her help save his catch. "You know, Olaf might be on to something," she said. "What if we help restore the harvest?"

"Yes! I can help restore the harvest!" Olaf exclaimed. "How do I do that?" he whispered to Elsa.

Elsa took Olaf by the hand and led him to the leader of the ice harvesters. "We're going to join the team," she explained.

"I've always wanted to be on a team!" Olaf said.

The foreman wasn't sure about Olaf. The snowman was very small compared to the rest of the workers. And Elsa and Anna had very little experience harvesting ice. But for his queen, he was willing to give it a try.

The ice harvesters carefully pulled the remaining sleds back onto the lake. They would have to start all over again, cutting new blocks of ice. Olaf scampered after them, trying to keep up on his stocky, snowy legs. Soon the ice harvesters picked a spot to begin again. They took out their long saws and began to carve the ice.

Kristoff, Anna, and Elsa followed their lead.

Olaf struggled to lift his saw. The blade was long and heavy. It was covered in sharp metal teeth that seemed to frown. "Cheer up, Mr. Saw," Olaf said.

Seconds later, he wedged the tip of the saw into the ice. Olaf looked very proud of himself. Now all he had to do was cut.

Olaf leaned against the handle and pushed as hard as he could, but the saw blade didn't budge. He hopped up and down and pressed with all his might. Still, nothing happened.

Kristoff noticed Olaf struggling and offered to help. He took Olaf's saw by the handle and pushed.

But Olaf must have wedged the saw into the ice at a strange angle. Instead of slicing through the ice, the saw blade bent double. Stunned, Kristoff let go. The saw snapped back with a loud *TWANG,* accidentally smacking Olaf in his carrot nose.

"Sorry," Kristoff said. But Olaf only giggled. He didn't seem to feel any pain.

"Maybe carving isn't your specialty," Elsa said. She gently led Olaf to the group of harvesters lifting ice blocks from the lake. Kristoff followed and handed the snowman a pair of tongs.

Olaf stumbled under the weight of the tongs, but at least they were lighter than the saw. He gazed at the newly cut blocks of ice floating on the surface of the lake.

"Hello, cousins!" he cried, waving to them. "Don't worry, this will be fun! Just like bobbing for apples!"

Olaf swung his tongs open and held them out with his tiny twig arms. He managed to grasp a large cube of ice. But Elsa knew ice, and ice was slippery. She winced as the tongs slid across the slick surface of the ice block and out of Olaf's hands. They fell into the lake with a splash!

Elsa, Anna, and Kristoff cringed. So far, the plan to restore the harvest was not going very well.

"Listen, why don't you help move the ice?" Elsa suggested. It seemed to be the safest job for Olaf. All he had to do was slide the ice blocks across the lake so that a worker could transfer them to a sled.

Olaf nodded eagerly and flexed his little arms, as he'd seen Kristoff do. He found a block of ice and pushed it across the slippery lake. It looked like a success. There were no heavy tools for him to break or lose. He seemed at one with nature.

From the banks of the lake, Elsa and Anna watched, relieved. Olaf had finally found a way to help. He hopped happily back and forth, sliding one block after another.

As the afternoon wore on, the sun moved out from behind the clouds. Its brilliant rays shone down on the ice harvesters. The thick ice covering the lake was starting to get a little slick. Most of the workers didn't seem to mind—their boots were built to keep them safe, and they were used to walking on slippery ice. Olaf had his personal flurry to keep him cool, but he didn't have boots on his snowy feet.

Anna noticed and tapped Elsa on the shoulder. "Is it just me, or is Olaf . . . slipping?" she asked.

Elsa stopped working and stared at Olaf. Anna was right. Olaf was starting to slide more with every step. Elsa could see that a thin layer of water was forming beneath his feet.

"Olaf!" Elsa called out. She wanted to

tell him to stand still until the workers could help him.

Olaf smiled back at them and waved cheerfully. Then he got right back to work. He didn't seem to understand why she was calling to him. He gave the next ice block a hearty shove. But instead of the ice block sliding away, Olaf started to slide in the other direction.

Elsa and Anna tried to run after him, but Anna slipped on the ice. She grabbed Elsa's arm as she slid toward Olaf.

The three of them crashed into a tall pile of ice, sending the blocks tumbling this way and that. The huge pieces fell down around them. Many cracked and split open against the frozen lake. Olaf was surrounded by big chunks of crunchy ice.

When the frost cleared, the ice harvesters were staring in shock. This was the second time today that their visitors had ruined the harvest.

Elsa looked out at the broken ice spread across the lake. She felt bad. It would take the workers days to make up the harvest, but if she used her powers, she could fix everything in moments. After all, ice was her specialty.

"Maybe I can help," Elsa said. She motioned for everyone to stand back.

Elsa raised her arms and summoned her magical powers. An icy wind swirled around her and ruffled her hair. She extended her hands into the frosty gale and then knelt to touch the surface of the lake.

The lake rumbled at Elsa's touch. The rumbling spread outward from beneath her fingers to the center of the lake. There, the ice began to split apart. But instead of cracking randomly, it split into perfect cubes.

The ice harvesters watched in wonder.

They'd never seen anything like this before. The ice blocks slowly came out of the water as a new surface of ice rose underneath them. It looked as though the ice was moving all by itself—but it was Elsa's magic.

In just a few minutes, the entire day's harvest was saved. The ice blocks were lined up in neat rows on top of the frozen lake. All the workers had to do was load the sleds. Elsa gently lowered her arms.

Anna beamed with pride. Olaf and Kristoff stared at her in admiration. They wore the same smiles as the ice harvesters, who gazed at Elsa, amazed. Her powers were a wonder to see.

"Thank you, Queen Elsa!" the foreman said.

"You're welcome," Elsa replied, nodding graciously. "I'm glad I could help. After all, what are queens for?"

The men bowed before her and then quite unexpectedly lifted her onto their shoulders. Elsa gasped, then grinned. This was fun!

"Three cheers for Queen Elsa!" they shouted heartily. "All hail the Queen!"

Chapter 5

When she woke the next morning, Elsa was still glowing with a sense of accomplishment. She'd saved the ice harvest, and the harvesters were happy. The good memory put a spring in her step as she dressed for the day. Elsa strolled through the halls of the palace, happily humming a tune to herself.

Just outside her study, Anna greeted her breathlessly.

"Ready for number five?" she asked, holding up her adventure list.

"Definitely," Elsa replied. "What's on the agenda?"

"A picnic with some friends I met in the village," Anna explained.

"That sounds wonderful," Elsa said. "Just let me grab my cloak. I think I left it in here."

Elsa opened the door to her study, expecting the usual early-morning quiet. Instead, she was surprised by a gaggle of voices coming from outside.

She turned to Anna for an answer, but

her sister looked as puzzled as she was.

Elsa crossed to the windows and looked out. A huge crowd of people had gathered in the courtyard.

"What is it?" Anna asked, coming up beside her.

"I'm not sure," Elsa said.

The sisters hurried downstairs, on the hunt for answers. They were met by Kai, the butler. He was busy directing a handful of servants.

"Kai, what's going on?" asked Elsa.

"The villagers are here to see you, Your Majesty," the butler explained.

"Why? Is something wrong?" Elsa asked anxiously.

"No, Your Majesty," Kai said,

chuckling. "They're seeking an audience with the queen. They want your help."

Kai led Elsa and Anna down the main corridor. He and the servants were getting the audience chamber ready. The audience chamber was a special room where the villagers could visit with the queen.

Outside the chamber, two footmen stood at the ready. They opened two grand doors as Elsa approached. She walked into the beautiful hall with the high ceilings and took her seat on the throne. Anna followed and stood beside her.

"We'll let the villagers in as soon as you're ready, Your Majesty," Kai said.

"All right," Elsa said. She was nervous and excited all at once. The people of the village were depending on her. She wrung her hands and noticed her sister standing beside the throne.

"I'm sorry, Anna. It looks like I won't be able to go to the picnic today," Elsa apologized.

"That's okay. Maybe we can reschedule," Anna said. "This is important." Elsa could tell that Anna understood, but she still looked disappointed.

"Don't do that," Elsa said. "You go ahead without me."

Anna hesitated. "Are you sure?"

Elsa nodded and then turned to Kai. "I'm ready," she said. "Let them in."

Moments later, a long line of people filed into the room. Anna stepped away from the throne as the villagers approached. She left the chamber quietly, following the line of people, which extended all the way through the palace courtyard into the village.

*

The first villager Kai brought before Elsa was a farmer named Niels. He grew grains and vegetables for the town.

"Good day, Your Majesty," he said, bowing deeply. "It's an honor to meet you."

"It's nice to meet you, too," Elsa said. "What brings you here?"

"Well, I heard what you did for the ice harvesters," Niels said. The other villagers in the room murmured with excitement.

"I was wondering if you could help me with my crop."

"What's the trouble with your crop?" she asked.

"Lately, we've had wonderful weather in Arendelle . . . for people," Niels explained. "But all those days of sunshine have been hard on my brussels sprouts."

"How can I help?"

"My sprouts taste much better after a thin coating of snow, Your Majesty," Niels said. "I thought you might be able to . . . you know." The farmer wiggled his fingers as if he were casting a spell.

Elsa was eager to help the villagers in any way she could. If that meant using her powers, she was happy to do it. But she couldn't just make it snow on the other side of the kingdom.

Elsa asked Kai to fetch a wagon. Then she stood and swirled her fingers through the air. She filled the wagon with a beautiful pile of fluffy snow.

"When you return home, just spread the snow around your fields," she said to Niels. "Will that help your vegetables?"

"Yes! Thank you, Your Majesty!" Niels said gratefully. "My crops will be happy for the water, too!" He bowed again before he left the chamber, happily pushing the wagon of snow.

The next villager in line was a piemaker named Tilda. She was thrilled to meet the queen, and greeted Elsa with her best

curtsy. All of the villagers in the room knew Tilda and loved her pies. That was the problem.

"I make a lot of pies, Your Majesty," Tilda explained. "But I have nowhere to keep them until they're sold. I used to place them on my windowsill, but the children would stick their thumbs in them."

"I'm sorry to hear that," Elsa said sympathetically.

"I don't like to leave them out anyhow," Tilda said. "If they sit too long, my banana creams spoil and my meringues melt."

Elsa frowned, puzzled by the dilemma. She wasn't a baker, but there had to be a way to keep the pies fresh. "What about an icebox?" she suggested.

"I would love an icebox," Tilda replied. "But I can't afford one. Besides, none of the iceboxes I've seen at any of the trading posts are large enough for all my pies."

Elsa knew what to do. She summoned her frosty powers and a chill whipped through the audience chamber. Tilda shivered, but not for long. Elsa quickly conjured a huge box made entirely of ice. The box glistened in the middle of the audience chamber. It was twice as big as the icebox in the royal kitchen. "Put your pies in this," Elsa said. "That should keep them fresh. Perhaps you could even pack the icebox in straw to make it last longer."

"Oh, thank you, Your Majesty!" Tilda said. "Now I have my very own icebox."

Elsa called for servants to help Tilda carry the box. The baker left with a smile on her face.

*

By now the sun was in the middle of the sky. It was afternoon, and Elsa had spent the entire morning helping the people of Arendelle. The villagers were very nice and very grateful, but she had to admit she was growing tired.

The next villager in line was a tall blond man with a funny accent.

"Hoo, hoo! My name's Oaken," he announced. "I run a trading post. Wandering Oaken's Trading Post and Sauna, *ja?*"

"Lovely to see you again, Oaken," Elsa replied. "How can I help you today?"

First Oaken offered the queen half off on a brand-new pair of snowshoes, and then he explained his troubles. He wanted to build an ice room for his customers. That way they could cool down quickly after the sauna.

"An entire room made out of ice? Are you sure?" Elsa asked.

"*Ja!*" Oaken said enthusiastically.

Elsa agreed. The cold had never bothered her. In fact, she preferred it. She and Oaken set to work drawing up plans for the ice room. They decided that Elsa would go to the trading post to help build it the next day.

"Hoo, hoo!" Oaken said as he dashed off. Elsa smiled. She could tell that for Oaken, "hoo, hoo" meant many things. One of them was "thank you."

Elsa gazed out across the audience chamber. The line of villagers still stretched into the courtyard. Even though she had spent half the day working, it looked as though she hadn't helped anyone at all. There were just as many people waiting for her now as there had been in the morning.

Elsa sighed. It was going to be a long afternoon. Most of all, she missed Anna.

Chapter 6

Meanwhile, Anna had reluctantly gone on the picnic without her sister. She met up with her new friends on a beautiful hillside in full bloom. Lise, Thea, and Sigrid had all grown up in the village. Anna had first met them on one of her first adventures in Arendelle.

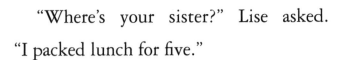

"Where's your sister?" Lise asked. "I packed lunch for five."

"She couldn't make it," Anna said. "She had some . . . queen stuff to do."

"Oh, that's too bad," Thea said. "I was looking forward to meeting her."

Sigrid spread a large patchwork blanket out on the grass. The four girls sat around Lise's picnic basket. They unpacked their lunch. The basket was full of sandwiches and delicious tarts. For dessert, Anna had brought flangendorfers.

"So, Anna, what's it like to live in the castle?" Sigrid asked. She lived on a dairy farm. Every morning she got up early and milked the cows. Then she helped her father deliver milk to the village.

"I guess it's not so different from living on a farm," Anna answered, placing a sandwich on her plate.

"Are you joking?" Thea asked. Her father was a fisherman. She spent a lot of time at sea with her brothers and sisters. "It's the castle! It's beautiful! I bet no one ever tells you to clean your room."

"That's not true," Anna laughed. "Kai tells me to clean my room all the time!"

"But you have servants!" said Lise. Her parents were merchants who traded for silk and spices.

"The servants help us take care of the palace, but we still have big responsibilities," Anna explained.

The girls chatted as they ate. The

midday sun was bright. They basked in the warm afternoon light.

"Does the castle get lonely sometimes?" Sigrid asked, curious.

Anna thought for a moment. There were times when the castle did get lonely. She thought of all those years Elsa had spent locked away from her, hiding her powers. "It can be," Anna said. "Don't get me wrong. I'm really lucky to live there. But I guess the most important thing isn't the castle; it's the people in it."

"What do you mean?" Lise asked.

Anna shrugged, searching for a way to explain. "Well, the castle's just a castle," she said. "It's my family that makes it a home."

"I think I understand," Thea said. "Without my brothers and sisters, the fishing boat wouldn't be the same."

"Yes!" Sigrid chimed in eagerly. "I can't imagine the farm without the cows!"

Lise laughed gently. "Are you sure you mean the cows, and not your family?" she asked Sigrid.

"The cows are family," Sigrid said seriously. "Besides, they never ask me to clean my room."

The four girls laughed.

Later, when the girls were finished eating, they stretched out on the picnic blanket. Anna, Lise, Thea, and Sigrid gazed up at

the fluffy white clouds floating across the sky.

I wish Elsa were here, Anna thought.

As if reading her thoughts, Lise asked, "So, what is your sister like?"

Anna plucked a bright green blade of grass and twirled it between her fingers. "Elsa's great," she replied. "She's funny, and she's smart. And she's creative. She even made this really cool ice palace once."

The more Anna thought about Elsa, the more she missed her. She wondered how things were going back at the palace.

"It can't be easy to be the queen," Lise said. "I bet there's a lot to do."

"Tell me about it!" Anna said. "When I left this morning, there was a whole line of people waiting for Elsa to help them."

"Who helps Elsa?" Thea asked.

Anna opened her mouth to answer, but then she closed it again. It was a good question. She wasn't sure she knew the answer. There were servants at the palace who could get Elsa anything she needed, but that wasn't exactly the same. Who was there to help her laugh? Who was there to help her rest? Who was there to help pick her up when she was down?

Anna grew worried. It was *her* job to help her sister, and she wasn't there.

Suddenly, the hillside darkened. The fluffy clouds that had been dancing across the sky only moments before had vanished. In their place were gray clouds.

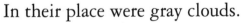

"Uh-oh, it looks like it's going to rain," Sigrid said.

Everyone stood and packed up the picnic. Anna had just finished helping Thea fold the blanket when a tiny snowflake floated down from the sky. Anna looked up. Yes, it was starting to

snow. She could see the flakes falling lightly on the castle.

"Does that usually happen?" Thea asked.

"Not at this time of year," Anna said, puzzled.

"Maybe it's a sign," Sigrid offered. The other girls gave her a doubtful look.

It sounded strange, but Anna wondered if Sigrid was right. Anna looked toward the castle again. Her eyes widened as she finally understood. Elsa needed her!

Chapter 7

Anna and her friends raced back to the castle. The closer they got to the castle, the heavier the snow became. When they got there, the crowd of villagers was still gathered in the courtyard. Some had pulled out umbrellas, while others held whatever they could find over their heads.

"Look at that line!" Lise exclaimed. "All those people are here to see the queen?"

"Looks that way," Anna said. She made her way through the crowd and into the castle. Her new friends followed.

In the audience chamber, Elsa was growing very tired. She'd used her powers all day, and it was finally starting to take a toll. She needed to rest and regain her strength, but she didn't want to let the people of Arendelle down.

Kai stood beside the throne. He glanced at Elsa with worried eyes.

"Maybe you should take a short break,

Your Majesty," he said gently.

"I can't, Kai," Elsa said. "The villagers are counting on me."

Even though Elsa was very tired, she did her best to smile. The next villager in line stepped forward and bowed to her.

"Your Majesty, are you okay?" he asked, concerned.

"I'm fine," she said faintly. "How can I help you?"

The villager looked doubtfully at the queen. She didn't look fine. Her face was pale, and there were dark circles under her eyes. Plus it had just started to snow *inside* the castle.

"It's okay, my queen," the villager said. "I'll come back some other time."

"No, wait—" Elsa began, but before she could finish her sentence, she collapsed. Instantly, the snow stopped and the clouds vanished.

"Elsa!" cried a voice. At the opposite end of the chamber, Anna had just arrived. She hurried over to the throne and scooped

Elsa up in her arms. Lise, Sigrid, and Thea looked on sympathetically. It definitely wasn't easy being the queen.

*

When Elsa woke the next morning, she thought she was still in the audience chamber. "How can I help you?" she murmured groggily.

Anna had been sitting patiently at her sister's bedside. When she saw that Elsa was awake, she jumped to her feet. "I'll tell you how you can help me. You can get some rest!" Anna ordered.

Elsa blinked slowly and sat up in bed. "Anna, you're here," she said softly.

"Of course I'm here," Anna replied.

"I was worried about you! When I saw the snow, I came back."

"The snow," Elsa echoed. Her features settled into an anxious frown. "Is everyone okay?" She threw back the covers and tried to stand. Anna gently pushed her back against the pillows.

"Everyone's fine," Anna said. "They just thought it was an unseasonable flurry, until it started snowing inside."

Embarrassed, Elsa covered her face with her hands. She hadn't meant for the snow to happen. Using her powers all day long had worn her out. "I just got so tired," she said.

"I know," Anna replied. "That's why you should take the day off."

"I can't. The people of Arendelle are depending on me," Elsa said. She climbed slowly to her feet. This time Anna didn't stop her. Elsa walked over to her wardrobe and pulled out a dress.

"Maybe there's a way you can help everyone without getting so tired," Anna suggested.

"I don't see how I could," Elsa said. "The villagers need me to use my powers." She thought of all the people she had helped the day before—all the wonderful things her powers had let her do. Until she'd gotten too tired, it had been fantastic.

"I get it," Anna said. "Your powers are very cool—literally! You can build palaces out of ice! You can send snowflakes whirling through the air and harvest an entire day's worth of ice in minutes. You really are a snow queen."

Elsa smiled.

"But you're also strong, and smart, and the world's best big sister," Anna added. "There are plenty of other ways for you to help the villagers. They don't need you to use your powers. Not all the time."

Elsa thought for a moment as she pulled on her dress. "But I'm good at it," she said. "I'm good at using my powers. It helps the people see that I'm not always so . . . queenly."

Elsa remembered Anna's impression of her in the square, waving stiffly to the villagers. Her sister had only been joking, but something about it rang true.

Sometimes Elsa didn't feel as close to the villagers as she wanted to. They were always so careful around her, bowing and apologizing for everything. Elsa tried her best to relate to them, but the distance was still there.

It was different for Anna. She could make a nervous young girl laugh and impress a pastry chef with a noisy belch. Elsa might have been the one with magical powers, but she didn't have Anna's people magic.

"Is that what this is about?" Anna asked. "You being queenly?"

Elsa nodded gloomily. "A little."

"Well, of course you're queenly! You're the queen! You can do anything, including helping people without using your powers!" Anna said.

Elsa's eyes brightened as she realized that Anna was absolutely right. She felt a burst of energy. She straightened her shoulders and headed for the bedroom door.

"Are you sure I can't convince you to take the day off?" Anna asked.

"And disappoint that crowd of people out there?" Elsa said, pointing to the villagers visible from her bedroom window. "No chance."

Elsa might be smart, she might be funny, and she might be the world's best

big sister. But she was also stubborn.
"Then I'm coming with you," Anna said,
determined.

Stubbornness ran in the family.

Chapter 8

In the audience chamber, the line of villagers was just as long as it had been the day before. Elsa took her seat on the throne and greeted the people of Arendelle. Anna stood beside her.

The first villager of the day was a fish merchant named Anders. He had heard about the magic icebox Elsa had given to Tilda the piemaker. "If it's not too much trouble, would Your Majesty make one for me?" he asked. Anders needed to keep his fish cold and fresh.

Elsa thought about it for a moment. "What if I have my royal carpenters build you a large icebox out of wood or stone?" she said. "You can buy ice blocks from the harvesters and put them inside the box to keep your fish cold."

It was a perfect solution, but Anders looked disappointed. "I was hoping you would make me a box with your magic," he said hopefully.

Elsa chewed her lip as she considered it. She hated to let Anders down. It would be so easy to use her powers, and it would make him happy. "Of course I can make you a box. It's no trouble at all," she said.

Elsa wove her hands through the air in a swirl of ice crystals. Anders and the villagers waiting in line gasped in awe. With a blast of frost and a whirl of icicles, Elsa built the box.

Anders thanked her wholeheartedly. Elsa called for servants to help him carry the icebox. The fish merchant left happy.

Elsa turned to the next villager, but not before Anna tugged on her sleeve.

"You didn't have to use your powers," Anna whispered.

"I know, but he really wanted me to," Elsa replied.

"Just don't overdo it," Anna said. "Remember, there are other ways to help people."

Elsa agreed and promised Anna that she'd be careful.

*

Morning slipped by quickly again, and before long, afternoon had arrived. Even though Elsa's plan had been to help the villagers without using her powers, it was harder than she'd thought it would be. She'd given in many times, to the delight of the villagers. But Elsa was starting to feel uneasy about it. Magic was just one

part of her, and if magic was all the people expected, they would never truly know her.

A seamstress named Dagmar curtsied in front of Elsa. She explained that she ran the village laundry. "Lately, there have been more and more dirty clothes, Your Majesty, and I can't get enough water to clean them," Dagmar said.

"I'm sorry to hear that," Elsa replied sympathetically. "How can I help?"

Dagmar and the laundry workers had to carry buckets of water back and forth. There was so much laundry, they couldn't carry the water fast enough. "Is there any way your magic could help with the water, Your Majesty?" she asked.

Elsa considered Dagmar's request. The seamstress seemed to be hoping for Elsa come up with some magical solution, but Elsa knew a different way. She glanced over at Anna and remembered her words. There were other ways to help the people of Arendelle. Elsa had more than her magic to offer.

"Wait here," she said.

Elsa stepped down from the throne and left the chamber. She raced through the palace to her study.

On the desk, her plans for Arendelle's new plumbing system were right where she'd left them two days before. She scooped up the papers and ran back to the audience room.

Elsa showed the plans to Dagmar. "The pipes and canals will carry water all across the village," she said. "We can run a pipe out to you and build a water pump. You'll be able to draw water right at the laundry."

Dagmar's eyes widened in excitement as she looked at the plans. "Do you think you can do this?" she asked hopefully.

"*We* can do this," Elsa replied. She turned to address the crowd gathered in the audience chamber. "This plumbing system will benefit everyone—farmers, fisherman, and piemakers alike. If everyone pitches in, we can build the water pump in a day! Who will help me?"

The villagers murmured to each other. Digging canals and laying pipes wasn't quite as fun as watching Elsa use her magic.

"I'll help!" Anna said, stepping forward. She took Elsa's hand and squeezed it in support.

"Me too!" Dagmar said.

"I'll help!" cried a farmer.

"Count me in!" said several merchants.

Word spread along the line of villagers to the crowd in the courtyard. One by one, the people of Arendelle agreed to lend a hand.

Chapter 9

The next day, Elsa, Anna and the villagers rose early. They set out at dawn with the palace builders, plumbers, and architects. All over town, the work began. The people of Arendelle dug canals and trenches for the new plumbing system.

Kristoff and the ice harvesters were the

first to break ground. Shoveling wasn't so different from ice carving. They worked together in a well-organized team, singing the songs of the frozen lake.

Even Olaf was given a special task. He helped Chef Florian serve refreshments to the hardworking villagers. Florian was also famous for his frosty lemonade.

"Fresh-squeezed lemonade!" Olaf cried, carrying a small tray of glasses.

"Is it cold?" asked a villager, wiping the sweat from his brow.

"Of course it's cold!" Olaf replied. "Thanks to my cousins!"

By early evening, the canals were finished and most of the pipes had been laid. At Dagmar's laundry, Elsa and Anna worked side by side. The sisters were up to their elbows in dirt, putting the finishing touches on a brand-new water pump.

Anna looked at Elsa and broke into a fit of giggles.

"What's so funny?" Elsa asked.

"You don't look so queenly now," Anna said. The hem of Elsa's dress was stained

with mud, there was dirt smeared across her cheek, and her brow was drenched with sweat.

"I look absolutely queenly," Elsa said. She lifted her chin defiantly. "This is what a queen looks like when she's working."

Anna straightened up and stretched. They'd spent most of the day hunched over, digging trenches.

Elsa paused and blew a sweaty lock of hair from her eyes. "You were right, Anna," she said. "I love using my magic to help people. But some days, helping them this way is even better."

"Way to win their hearts," Anna said, smiling.

Elsa slid the pump handle into place

and called to Dagmar. The seamstress put down her shovel and hurried over to the queen.

"Why don't you give it a try," Elsa told Dagmar.

"Yeah," Anna said. "Let's see if this thing we built actually works."

Dagmar gripped the handle and lifted it up, then pushed it down. A strange gurgling noise rumbled through the pipes. Dagmar took that as a sign of encouragement and pumped faster. Suddenly, water spilled from the spout. It was cold and clear and fresh.

Dagmar was thrilled. She turned to Elsa with tears of joy in her eyes. "I don't know how to thank you!" she cried.

"I do," Anna said. "Three cheers for Queen Elsa!"

A cheer went up among the villagers. They gathered around and lifted Elsa up onto their shoulders.

"All hail the Queen!" the people of Arendelle shouted.

Chapter 10

A few days later, Elsa got up, dressed, and made her way to the audience chamber. The people of Arendelle were enjoying their new water system. That particular problem had been solved, but they still came to Elsa for guidance, and she enjoyed helping them. The difference was that they didn't expect her to use her powers. Now they knew her better.

Elsa opened the doors to the audience chamber and was surprised to find it empty. Just then, Anna walked up beside her.

"I hope you don't mind, but I gave the villagers the day off," Anna said with a grin.

"The villagers don't need a day off," Elsa replied.

"But you do," she said.

"Anna, we've been over this. You know I have responsibilities. The people of Arendelle are depending on me," Elsa explained.

"I know. That's why Kai and I have

125

worked out a schedule. The people of Arendelle will visit the palace three days a week. The other days are for your other duties, like spending time with your sister," Anna said.

Elsa started to protest but realized there was no reason to. It was a brilliant idea. It gave her time to do everything she wanted, especially spend time with Anna. That was the hardest part about those long hours in the audience chamber—it was time spent away from her sister.

"So what's next on the list?" Elsa asked.

"You mean this list?" Anna said, pulling the scroll from her pocket. She unrolled her list of Things to Do in Arendelle. "We're up to number six."

"Let me guess, more flangendorfers," Elsa joked.

"Heavens, no!" Anna said dramatically. "Number six is going to be our biggest adventure yet."

Elsa raised an eyebrow. "What's that?" she asked doubtfully.

"Sisterly bonding," Anna said.

"Piece of cake," Elsa told her.

The two sisters clasped hands and strolled through the halls of the palace. They walked out into the courtyard, ready for their next adventure . . . together.

For Quinn —E.D.

Disney
Anna & Elsa

#2: Memory and Magic

By Erica David

Illustrated by Bill Robinson

Random House New York

Chapter 1

"One, two, three!" Princess Anna of Arendelle shouted. Her feet were perched at the edge of a floating slab of ice. The ice floe bobbed through the rapids of Odin's Fjord, an icy waterway. The narrow lane of water had steep banks made of stone. At the count of three, Anna leaped from one patch of ice to another.

"Anna, be careful!" Elsa called from the royal barge. But there was no stopping her younger sister. Even though Elsa was queen and ruled the village, there were times when it seemed that Anna was really the one in charge. She had been out of the boat and on the ice before anyone had the chance to try to talk her out of it.

"Careful is my middle name!" Anna replied.

"Really?" Elsa asked doubtfully. "The last time I checked, it was Not Nearly Careful Enough!"

Anna skipped back and forth across the floating sheets of ice. When she landed on an ice floe next to the royal barge, she hopped on board, joining her sister.

"You know that I could use magic to help you?" Elsa asked her. "I could freeze the water under your feet."

"It's more fun this way!" Anna insisted.

The barge they stood on was a long, slow-moving boat. *Too slow,* Anna thought. Normally, it was used to transport goods to neighboring villages. Today, Elsa had suggested they take it on a tour of the fjords.

Anna had been enjoying the tour, but she thought it could use a little more action. When she saw the swirling rapids, she knew it was the perfect place to try ice hopping. And she was right. She loved the thrill of jumping from one sheet of ice to the next. The bubbling currents of the fjord made for an exciting challenge.

"Your turn!" Anna said to Elsa.

Elsa gazed out at the choppy waves. "I don't know, Anna . . . ," she said hesitantly. "It looks fun, but I think I'll pass."

"You'll be fine," Anna told her. "Besides, we made a deal. I try something you like, you try something I like."

"Are you sure this is what you like?" asked Elsa. She watched the ice floes bob and dip on the current.

"Positive," Anna said. "And no magic!"

Elsa squared her shoulders and took a deep breath. She got ready to take the plunge. Actually, the point was *not* to plunge. The point was to land safely on the ice. Elsa jumped off the deck.

"Your Majesty!" the boat captain cried in alarm.

"It's okay, Klaus," Anna said. "She meant to do that."

Elsa landed easily on a patch of ice. She looked unsure, but she was safe and sound. She found her balance as the ice floated on the choppy water. After a moment, she hopped to the next sheet of ice drifting downstream.

Elsa leaped from floe to floe for a few moments and quickly returned to the barge. As she climbed on deck, Anna congratulated her.

"Not bad for your first time ice hopping," she said.

"I think it'll be my last," Elsa replied.

"You didn't like it?" Anna asked.

"It's definitely exciting," Elsa answered. "But maybe a little *too* thrilling for my taste."

Anna snorted at the word "taste." The day before, it had been Anna's turn to try something Elsa liked. Elsa had decided she wanted her sister to eat pickled herring, her favorite fish. Anna had hated the smell of it as a child, so she never ate it. Elsa thought it was high time for Anna to give it another try.

*

When the castle chef had set the large platter of fish in front of Anna that day, she'd wrinkled her nose. *Pickled herring*

has a funny smell, she thought. The scent drifted through the dining room. Anna's stomach lurched.

Reluctantly, she placed a tiny piece of fish on her plate. Elsa had already started eating. She'd been looking forward to the meal all day. She gazed at Anna expectantly.

Anna speared a forkful of fish and brought it to her lips. The trouble was she didn't want to open her mouth.

"Don't be so dramatic," Elsa said. "The worst that could happen is that you don't like it."

"I'm not so sure. What if this fish pickles my insides?" Anna joked.

Elsa smiled patiently.

Slowly, Anna opened her mouth. She

tucked the fish inside and squeezed her lips shut. She chewed quickly. The faster she chewed it, the less time she had to taste it. Finally, Anna managed to swallow it down.

"So, what do you think?" Elsa asked.

"It's just as weird as I thought it would be," Anna said.

"Weird? Pickled herring is the cook's specialty!" said Elsa.

Anna shrugged. "Sorry," she said. "But I *especially* don't like it." She wrinkled her nose again. "How can you eat this stuff?"

Elsa didn't reply. She simply shoveled another forkful into her mouth. She smiled with pleasure as she gobbled it

down. Judging by the look on her face, one would think pickled herring was the most delicious food in the world. It was clear that Anna and her sister had very different tastes.

Back on the boat, Anna was surprised that Elsa didn't love ice hopping as much as she did. It was so much better than eating pickled fish.

"Instead of trying things only one of us likes, let's find something we both like to do," Anna said.

"I have the perfect idea," Elsa told her.

That night, the sky over Arendelle was

filled with stars. The Northern Lights shimmered in the distance. They were so bright they lit up the entire village.

Anna and Elsa were sitting comfortably in the back of a beautiful sleigh. The royal coachman was taking them for a ride under the stars.

"This was a wonderful idea," Anna said.

"I thought you'd like it," Elsa replied. "There's no pickled herring in sight."

Anna laughed. She glanced at Elsa. These past few weeks, they had been spending more and more time together. They had gone ice fishing with Kristoff and paid a visit to Oaken's sauna.

Anna realized that it didn't matter what kind of adventure they had. As long as she and Elsa were together, they had fun. It had been that way even when they were little girls. In Anna's earliest memories, she and Elsa played together all the time.

Anna felt happy when she thought of those childhood days. But when she tried to recall specific things, she only remembered laughter and snow. In the sleigh under the beautiful winter sky, Anna furrowed her brow. There had to be more than just laughter and snow. She was sure of it.

"What's wrong?" Elsa asked, noticing her sister's expression.

"Nothing," Anna said. "Remember how we used to play together as girls?"

"Yes," Elsa replied, smiling.

Anna chewed her lower lip. There was something nagging at her.

"Well, I'm not sure I do," she said uneasily.

Chapter 2

The next morning, Anna tried to shake off the strange feeling from the night before. She'd only been tired, she told herself. She had so many memories of good times with Elsa, it was hard to keep track. That was all. She was sure the details would come back to her.

Anna and Elsa took a walk in the woods with Kristoff, Sven the reindeer, and Olaf the snowman. It was the perfect winter morning—crisp, cold, and made for a snowball fight. Anna grabbed a handful of fresh snow and made a ball. She lobbed it at Kristoff, who pulled a face like he was angry, then smiled. He chased Anna through the trees and pelted her with snowballs.

Olaf ran straight for Elsa. He hurled himself at her knees. The snowman playfully tried to knock her over.

"Olaf! No tackling. This is a snowball fight!" Elsa exclaimed. "You're supposed to throw snowballs!"

"But I *am* snowballs! I'm made of snow!" Olaf explained cheerfully. "I just threw myself!"

Elsa laughed and climbed to her feet. She dusted the snow from her skirts. "I think that's an unfair advantage," she said.

"Oh. I never thought of that," Olaf said. "Truce?"

"Truce," Elsa agreed.

"How about a warm hug to seal the deal?" Olaf suggested. Olaf loved warm hugs.

"Sure," Elsa replied. She leaned down and hugged the little snowman. Olaf was delighted.

With Kristoff on her heels, Anna ran back to the clearing and saw Elsa and Olaf hugging. Something about the situation tugged at her memory. Olaf asked for warm hugs all the time, but that wasn't it. She tried to remember building a snowman

with Elsa when they were younger. They
must have built snowmen together. But
Anna couldn't remember exactly. The
more she tried to recall, the more confused
she became. All she could remember was
snow and laughter.

"Elsa, we've built snowmen together,
haven't we?" Anna asked.

"Of course," Elsa replied.

"It's funny. I can't seem to remember," said Anna.

Elsa grew quiet. "I'm sure you will soon," she said.

"It's kind of weird, though," Anna said, scratching her head. "Why would I forget something like that?"

"Maybe you're getting old," Olaf said brightly.

"I'm not getting old!" Anna exclaimed.

Elsa looked away. Anna had the strangest feeling that her sister knew something about her memory problem. For some reason, Elsa didn't want to tell her what she was thinking.

Kristoff was standing beside Anna,

petting Sven. Sven looked from Elsa to Anna and back again with a worried expression. Kristoff pretended to speak for Sven in a silly voice.

"'Gee, Kristoff. Why is everyone standing around awkwardly talking when there's a snowball fight going on?'

"I don't know, Sven," Kristoff replied in his normal voice. "Maybe they're scared to lose!"

Kristoff resumed the fight, hurling snowballs at Anna and Elsa. Both sisters ducked and ran for cover. Anna forgot her worries as she dodged the flying snow.

But once Elsa was safely behind a tree, she didn't rejoin the snowball fight. She only watched. Every time Anna ducked a

snowball, she thought she saw her sister wince. It was strange—Elsa usually loved snowball fights.

Anna raced past and pelted her sister with snow. Elsa halfheartedly tossed a snowball in return. The snowball brushed Anna's head lightly, and Anna fell to the ground in mock distress. She was only joking, not hurt at all, but Elsa froze. Her face went pale with horror. She stopped playing.

"Elsa, are you all right?" Anna asked, concerned.

"I . . . I'm okay," Elsa said. But Anna could tell it wasn't true. Something was bothering her sister. "I just remembered I have to go back to the castle."

"But you don't have any appointments today!" Anna protested.

"I know. I just . . . forgot something," Elsa told her.

"We'll all go back. We'll take my sleigh," Kristoff said.

"No, really, that's okay," Elsa insisted. "You all stay and have fun. I'll walk."

Anna stared at her sister, puzzled. It wasn't like Elsa to forget anything that had to do with castle business. The only one who seemed to be forgetting was Anna.

There's something strange going on here, Anna thought. She watched as Elsa walked off alone, headed for the castle. *And I'm going to get to the bottom of it.*

Chapter 3

The next day, Anna went for a walk in the forest. Usually, she would have asked Elsa to join her. But today she felt like being alone. She wanted time to think.

Anna was still worried about her foggy childhood memories. She couldn't seem to remember anything specifically related to Elsa's magic. It was very strange. She knew Elsa had been born with her powers.

She'd had them ever since they were little. But all of Anna's memories of Elsa's magic were very recent. They took place when Elsa was queen.

Anna spent the whole morning thinking about Elsa's magic. Something about it just didn't add up. She needed to speak to Elsa directly and ask her a few questions.

Anna was on her way back to the castle when suddenly, a large rock rolled into her path. The rock tumbled end over end and came to a stop at her feet. Then it popped open! Arms and legs and a shaggy head sprang out. Anna realized it wasn't a rock at all—it was a mountain troll!

"Greetings, my lady," the troll said. He had gray skin the same color as a stone.

A tuft of grass sprouted from the top of his head between two large, round ears.

"Hello," Anna said, surprised. She'd met some of the trolls before with Kristoff, but she didn't recognize this one. She'd never seen a troll during the daytime, either.

"My name is Brock," he said with a sweeping bow. "Brock the Mystical."

"Pleased to meet you, Brock the Mystical," Anna said. "I'm—"

"I know exactly who you are, Princess Anna. Anna the Beauteous!" he exclaimed.

Anna chuckled. "My name's not Anna the Beauteous," she told him. "Just Anna."

"All right, Just Anna," Brock said. He smiled widely at her, waggling his fuzzy

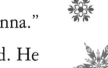

eyebrows. "I think I can be of service to you, my lady."

"How?" Anna asked.

"I have many magical powers," Brock explained.

"Oh, powers," Anna said. "My sister has those. She had a little trouble with them at first."

"No trouble here, Just Anna," Brock replied.

Anna looked doubtfully at the little troll. He seemed friendly enough, but she still wondered if he might be up to something.

"Look, I should be getting back to the castle," Anna said. She stepped around Brock and started to walk away.

"Aren't you forgetting something, my lady?" Brock asked.

"I don't think so," Anna said.

"Are you sure? What about your memories?"

Anna stopped. She turned to face the troll. "What do you know about my memories?" she asked.

"If you'd like to come with me, I'll show you," he replied.

Anna thought about it, then agreed. Maybe Brock could help her solve the mystery of her missing memories. She followed him deeper into the forest.

Brock led Anna along a winding path bordered by huge trees. They walked across a small stone bridge over a babbling creek. On the bank of the creek was a wide clearing, empty of snow and dotted with piles of dried leaves and brush. In the middle stood a little thatched hut made of grasses and twigs. It had a round, wooden door not much taller than Brock himself. Anna had to duck as she followed the troll into the hut.

"Welcome to my humble home, Just Anna," Brock said.

There wasn't much in the hut. There was a small fire pit in the middle of the room. A bed made of feathers and grass sat in one corner. There were several stacks of moldy books and a few old pots and pans. Other than that, the place was bare.

"May I offer you some birchbark tea, my lady?" Brock asked, lighting a fire in the pit.

"No thanks," Anna said. She was eager to learn what Brock knew about her memories.

Once they sat down, Brock began his tale. He told Anna how the trolls were the oldest creatures in Arendelle—older than the trees! They knew all the secrets of the forest. The oldest of them, the elder troll, was a powerful healer and artist.

Anna knew an elder troll. His name was Grand Pabbie. He'd told her how to thaw a frozen heart. Grand Pabbie was very wise.

"I'll let you in on a little troll secret," Brock said. "I'm going to be just like Grand Pabbie. My powers are growing every day." He picked up a pot and held it to his ear, as if it were talking.

"Oh," Anna said, watching Brock carefully. "So what do you know about my memories?"

"Your childhood memories of magic were removed," Brock explained.

The troll went on to describe a night long ago, when little Anna and her family had traveled to the mountains to see Grand Pabbie.

Elsa had accidentally zapped her sister with a magical swirl of ice while they were playing. Their parents had rushed Anna to the trolls.

Luckily, Grand Pabbie, the troll elder, had healed Anna. But the king and queen were afraid that people would not understand Elsa's powers. To keep them a secret, Grand Pabbie removed Anna's memories of Elsa's magic. He left only her memories of having fun.

That had all been a long time ago. Elsa didn't have to hide her powers anymore.

But Anna's memories of her sister's magic were still missing!

Anna was stunned as she listened to this tale. "That's impossible," she said.

Again, she thought about growing up with Elsa. Anna remembered certain things, like catching frogs together and singing in the bathtub. But when she tried to think of anything related to magic, all she remembered was snow and laughter. Brock's story made sense.

"Not to worry, Just Anna," Brock said. "I can bring back your memories."

Anna wasn't sure. Brock seemed nice enough, but he didn't seem very wise.

Even more troubling was the thought that if Brock was right, then Elsa knew what had happened. She had been there when their parents had taken Anna to Grand Pabbie. But Elsa would have told Anna about that . . . wouldn't she? Anna realized that even though they had spent a lot of time together lately, the sisters had not talked about their childhood very much.

Anna stood and bumped her head on the low ceiling of the hut. "I'm sorry," she said, rubbing her head. "But I have to go now."

Brock scrambled to his feet. "What about your memories, my lady? Surely you'll be wanting them back?"

Anna shook her head. She didn't know

what to believe. Slowly, she backed out of Brock's hut.

The troll looked disappointed, but he didn't give up. "Okay, Just Anna!" Brock called. "If you change your mind, you know where to find me!"

Chapter 4

Anna hurried toward the castle. She had
a lot of questions for Elsa. If her memories
of magic really had been removed, why
hadn't Elsa told her?

As Anna raced across the fields not
far from the castle, she passed a barn
where she knew Kristoff liked to putter.
Through the window, she saw that he was
inside. Anna stopped running. Kristoff

had grown up among the trolls. He had to know something about Brock and his story.

Anna slid open the barn door and hurried inside. Sven greeted her warmly. He nuzzled her pockets in search of carrots. Kristoff looked up from where he was polishing his sleigh.

"Don't you knock?" Kristoff asked, and then smiled.

"You're right. Where are my manners," Anna replied. She walked over to Kristoff and knocked on his sleigh.

"Hey! That's a fresh coat of lacquer!" Kristoff said.

Anna folded her arms across her chest.

"Are you ever going to actually ride in that sleigh or just polish it?" she asked.

"I ride in it all the time," he said. "That's why it needs fresh lacquer!"

Sven snorted at the two of them. The reindeer knew the only reason Anna and Kristoff pretended to argue was because they liked each other.

Anna cleared her throat. She decided to

start over. "I was hoping you could help me out," she said gently.

"Sure," Kristoff said, blushing. "What do you need help with?"

Anna told Kristoff about meeting Brock in the forest. She repeated the story the little troll had told her about the night her parents had taken her to Grand Pabbie. "So what do you think?" she asked when she was finished.

"What do I think about what?" Kristoff replied guardedly. Anna noticed that he was avoiding her gaze. He turned back to his sleigh and started polishing again.

"Is it true? About Grand Pabbie changing my memories? About Elsa not wanting to tell me?" Anna asked.

Kristoff shrugged. Anna walked around in front of him. He shifted so that he was facing away from her.

"You know something, don't you?" Anna said. She looked at him carefully.

"Who, me? Nope," Kristoff answered. Sven snorted again. Kristoff shot him a warning look. Sven snorted once more and turned away. "We know absolutely nothing."

Anna didn't believe it. She walked over to Sven.

"I know, Sven," she said. "Kristoff's hiding something."

"No, I'm not!" Kristoff responded a little too quickly.

Anna looked at Kristoff, then at Sven,

then back at Kristoff. Maybe there was a way for her to find out what Kristoff knew—and have a little fun while she was at it.

Anna stepped away from Sven and slid the barn door shut with a loud *THUD!* Kristoff jumped at the sound. Anna slammed the shutters closed over the windows. Suddenly, the barn was dark, except for the light of a single candle.

"Have a seat," she told Kristoff. She motioned to a chair at a small table in the corner.

Kristoff gripped his polishing rag in his fingers. He sat down at the table. Anna crossed her arms and started to pace behind him.

"True or false, you were raised by trolls?" she asked.

"Uh, true," Kristoff answered. The trolls had taken him in when he was very little. They were his family.

"True or false, you are an ice harvester?" Anna said.

"True," Kristoff replied, dropping his shoulders. He was beginning to relax.

This was all part of Anna's plan. She was going to start with the easy questions. Once Kristoff felt comfortable, she'd ask the tough ones.

"True or false," Anna said. "You know Grand Pabbie, the elder troll."

"Of course I know Grand Pabbie," Kristoff told her. At this third easy question, his face relaxed into a smile. "Grand Pabbie and I go way back."

"Since you were a little boy?" Anna continued.

Kristoff nodded.

"So you were there when Grand Pabbie changed my memories?" Anna asked casually.

"Yeah, sure I was. He just—" Kristoff stopped. "I mean—" He clapped his hands over his mouth and shook his head.

Sven snorted. "Quiet, you!" Kristoff barked.

"Let the reindeer speak!" Anna cried. Both Sven and Kristoff looked at her, puzzled. "You know what I mean!" she said. Although Anna was having fun teasing Kristoff, she also really wanted to know what he knew.

"I have ways of making you talk . . . ," she said playfully. She held up her hands as though she was going to start tickling him.

Kristoff clamped his mouth shut. He shook his head again.

Anna propped her hands on her hips. She studied her friend's face. She knew exactly how to get to him.

Anna walked over to Kristoff's sleigh. "Will you look at that?" she said to no one in particular. "What a beautiful sleigh. Is that a fresh coat of lacquer?" Anna took a measured step closer to the sleigh.

Kristoff sat up straight in his chair. His eyes grew wide.

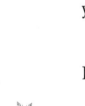

Anna licked a finger and touched it to the fresh lacquer. She smudged the shiny surface.

"Hey!" Kristoff cried. "That's my new sleigh!" He covered his eyes with his hands.

"I told you I'd make you talk!" Anna teased.

Kristoff uncovered his eyes and hung his head. After a moment, he looked up at Anna. It seemed like he was finally going to tell the truth, but then his expression changed. "Listen," he said. "It's not what you think. You should talk to your sister."

So it is true, Anna thought. Grand Pabbie had changed her memories. He'd made it so that she couldn't remember Elsa's magic, and Elsa had known all along!

Anna's face fell. Just when she thought everything was getting back to normal, she discovered another secret.

Chapter 5

Anna wandered through the halls of the castle looking for Elsa. Part of her wanted to find her sister right away. She had so many questions! But another part of her didn't want to see Elsa at all. Everything that had happened that day just made her feel so confused.

Anna found Elsa in the Hall of Portraits. It was a long corridor filled with paintings of Arendelle's royal family. There were portraits of the former king and queen, Elsa and Anna's parents. Next to those portraits were paintings of Anna and Elsa as young girls.

Anna looked at the eight-year-old version of herself in the painting. She was smiling from ear to ear. That girl had no idea that some of her most important memories were missing.

Elsa turned and spotted Anna at the end of the hall. "There you are," Elsa said. "I was looking for you."

"I took a walk," Anna said. She turned away from Elsa as she approached.

"Anna, what's wrong?" Elsa asked, worried.

Anna hadn't been sure that she wanted to talk to Elsa. But as soon as she started to talk, it all came out.

She told her sister about her foggy memories. She told her about meeting the strange little troll in the forest. She told her the story Brock had told Anna about why her memories were missing. And she told her how it seemed that Kristoff knew what had happened.

"Did you know, too?" Anna asked.

"Anna, I'm sorry," Elsa said. Anna could see that she felt awful. "I had no choice but to hide my powers when we were little. But I have a choice now. I should have told you about Grand Pabbie's magic."

"Why didn't you?" Anna asked.

"It's just hard for me to talk about that night," Elsa said.

It hit Anna all at once. Of course Elsa didn't like to talk about the night her powers had hurt Anna. They'd almost lost each other!

"It wasn't your fault! I know you didn't mean to hurt me," Anna said, suddenly wanting to comfort her sister. She knew Elsa loved her. "But it's really strange to know that some of my past is gone. It's like a part of me is missing."

Anna hung her head. She wasn't angry with Elsa. Instead, she was sad. "I can't remember your magic, Elsa," she said glumly.

Elsa placed an arm around her sister.

"Maybe I can help you remember," she said.

"How?" Anna asked.

Elsa took Anna by the hand and led her to her room. Once inside, Elsa opened a chest at the foot of her bed. The chest held all of Elsa's keepsakes. There was a beautiful shawl given to her by their mother, her favorite childhood doll, and a special book of nursery rhymes.

Elsa set those items aside and continued to look through the chest. Next, she found a note Anna had written when she was six. The giant letters were slanted across the page. The note read *Do you wanna build a snowman?*

Elsa put the note down on the bed and kept searching. Finally, she found what she was looking for. At the bottom of the chest was a small silk pouch. Elsa emptied the pouch into the palm of her hand. Anna

gasped. There sat the most incredible piece of magical ice. There was a beautiful glass crystal frozen inside. It shimmered in the light of Elsa's room.

"Do you remember how we got this?" Elsa asked.

Anna shook her head. Elsa placed the ice crystal in Anna's hand. Then she shared her favorite memory.

Elsa would never forget the day she and Anna got their first toboggan. Their father, the King of Arendelle, had given it to them as a present.

The beautiful wooden sled had a flat

bottom. The front curved up in a delicate curl.

The king took the girls into the snowy mountains. They spent all day sledding down the steep hills. Anna and Elsa loved the toboggan so much, they wanted to keep it inside the castle with them. They even wanted the toboggan to come to dinner.

"Please!" five-year-old Anna begged her parents. "Mr. Toboggan needs to eat!"

The king and queen told the girls that the toboggan didn't need to eat. It wasn't real. It could stay outside in the carriage house with the other sleds.

Anna was disappointed, but eight-year-old Elsa knew a way to cheer her up. The next morning, before their parents woke up, Anna and Elsa crept out of bed. Elsa took Anna's hand and led her to the top of the grand staircase.

Anna rubbed her eyes sleepily. "What are we doing, Elsa?" she asked.

"Shhh! I know a way we can toboggan inside," Elsa whispered.

Anna perked up. "Is Mr. Toboggan here?" she said excitedly.

"No, but I have a better idea," Elsa replied. She closed her eyes and concentrated. A cool snow flurry rippled through the room.

Anna hugged herself to keep warm. But Elsa knew her sister didn't mind the chill. It meant Elsa was about to use her powers.

Elsa opened her eyes. She waved her

fingers through the air. Frost formed at her fingertips.

With a twirl of her hands, she created a toboggan out of pure, clear ice. The sled sparkled and glistened. Anna gasped in amazement. She hurried over to the sled and climbed in.

Elsa twirled her hands again. A huge ramp of ice formed in front of her. The ramp ran down the staircase and wound through the halls of the castle.

"That's incredible!" Anna exclaimed.

Elsa pushed the ice sled to the top of the ramp and climbed on behind Anna. "Hold on tight!" she said.

The toboggan sailed down the ramp with a *WHOOSH!* Elsa and Anna squealed with

delight. The air rushed past them, whiffling through their hair.

They tobogganed through the castle halls from one room to the next. They sped through the kitchens and barreled through the library. The icy path twisted and turned through the corridors.

As they sped along the ramp, Anna saw that it ended in a giant loop-the-loop. Her fingers gripped the front of the sled.

"Get ready!" Elsa said.

Elsa and Anna huddled together. The sled approached the loop. It flew forward, and everything was upside down! They sailed through the loop and slid to a stop.

"Woo-hoo!" Anna cried. "This is amazing!"

Elsa laughed joyfully. She'd never had so much fun!

The ice ramp ended in the castle's ballroom. The sisters scrambled from the sled. They dusted the snow off their nightgowns. Elsa looked around at the enormous dance floor. Suddenly, she had an idea.

Elsa twirled her fingers and summoned her icy powers. A magical frost settled over the floor and hardened into a smooth sheet of ice. It was the perfect surface for ice-skating, or better yet, for playing hockey! Anna dashed off to grab her ice skates and Elsa found two wooden oars to use as sticks. They returned to the ballroom and Anna laced up.

"Elsa, we forgot the puck!" Anna said.

"Not to worry," Elsa answered. She grabbed a candy dish off the mantel, used her powers to cover it in ice, and dropped it to the floor. Elsa slapped the puck with her oar. It glided across the ballroom floor with ease. Anna clapped gleefully.

"My turn! My turn!" she said.

Anna pushed off from the wall and skated after the puck. When she reached it, she drew back and took a shot at Elsa's goal, the ballroom doorway behind her. Elsa skated forward and blocked her little sister's shot. Just like that, the game had begun! The sisters skated for what seemed like hours. They were having so much fun that they lost track of time.

"ELSA! ANNA! Where are you?" cried the queen from upstairs.

Elsa stopped skating. *Uh-oh,* she thought. She put a finger to her lips, motioning for Anna to be quiet, but Anna was in midswing. She slapped the puck with all her might. It bounced off her stick with a loud *crack* and hurtled through the air. The puck stuck the ballroom's fancy chandelier, knocking loose a tiny crystal.

"Oh, no!" Anna whispered.

Elsa reached out with her powers and zapped the crystal. She sealed it in a magical piece of ice.

When it hit the ground, it didn't break. It bounced right into Elsa's hands.

Elsa held the crystal up to the light. A

rainbow of colors danced through it. Anna stared at it in wonder.

Elsa tucked the crystal into Anna's pocket. "It's our secret," she said, taking Anna's hand. Anna smiled up at her big sister.

The ramp melted quickly, along with the sheet of ice on the ballroom floor. Together, Elsa and Anna hurried upstairs to meet their mother.

When Elsa finished her tale, she was smiling from ear to ear. She looked as happy and relaxed as Anna had ever seen her. "I'd forgotten how much fun it is to remember," she admitted. "Thank you for reminding me."

"Thank you, Elsa," Anna said quietly. It felt as though her sister had just returned a piece of her childhood. She was eager to remember more of their time together. She was eager to remember the magic. "Is there any way you can use your powers to get my memories back?" Anna asked.

Elsa shook her head sadly. "I'm sorry, Anna, but I can't. It's not my type of magic," she explained.

Anna nodded, but she wasn't going to give up so easily. After hearing Elsa's story and seeing how happy it made her to think

about it, Anna was more determined than ever. Those memories belonged to her, too. She had to find a way to get them back for herself!

Anna closed her fingers around the ice crystal in her palm. She vowed to get her memories back, one way or another. . . .

Chapter 6

The next morning, Anna was still thinking about Elsa's story. She couldn't believe it had been erased from her memory! She remembered sledding with Elsa, and she remembered that it was fun, but that was nothing compared to the magical adventures Elsa remembered. It was an experience the sisters had shared, but only Elsa remembered the magic.

That was why Anna had come up with a plan overnight. She called it Operation Remember the Time.

The first part of Anna's plan led her to the castle library. She searched the shelves and found old family histories and journals. Anna flipped through the books, hoping they would help her remember.

There were accounts of the young princesses written by friends and relatives. There were several tales of Princess Elsa as a little girl. But there weren't any hints of her magic in the stories, other than her love of playing outside in the snow.

The ones about Anna told the story of a baby eager to walk, talk, and explore. She was always crawling off in search of

adventure, and playing with her big sister.

It was wonderful to read through the family histories. Anna spent the whole morning in the library. But as afternoon approached, she was no closer to remembering.

It was time to move on to Part Two of her plan. Part Two was a return to the Hall of Portraits. Anna entered the long hallway. She stared at the paintings of her family members and ancestors. They dated back hundreds of years.

Anna walked slowly from portrait to portrait. She thought tracing her family's history might bring back some memories. She squinted and peered at the serious faces. She even recited the name of each person aloud. It was no use. Her memories of magic were still missing.

So far, Operation Remember the Time wasn't going anywhere. Anna sighed in frustration. But she wasn't done yet—she had arrived at the third and final part of her plan.

"Anna, wait!" Elsa called after her sister.

Anna marched through the halls of the castle and into the courtyard. "I have to, Elsa," she said. "If there's a chance I can get my memories back, I shouldn't waste it!"

Elsa hitched up her skirts and hurried after her sister. "But what do you really know about Brock?" she asked, concerned.

"Well, he's a troll, and trolls are magical," Anna replied.

Elsa raised an eyebrow. "That doesn't exactly sound like the best reason to trust someone."

Anna knew Elsa was probably right. Trolls were often up to mischief, and sometimes even spoke in mysterious riddles. But she had to try.

"I'm going, Elsa!" Anna said, determined. She left the courtyard and cut across the fields to the left of the castle.

"Then I'm going with you!" Elsa shouted. She ran after Anna and fell into step alongside her. Soon they walked by the barn, where Kristoff was working on his sleigh. When Kristoff saw them, he hurried outside and stood in their path.

"Hey, you!" he cried, pointing at Anna. "It took me all night to get that smudge out of the lacquer!" He cracked a smile. Kristoff was teasing her.

"Not now, Kristoff!" Anna said. She lifted her chin defiantly. "I'm on a mission."

"The last time you were on a mission, I lost my sled," Kristoff joked.

"Actually, I was hoping you could help us," Elsa said. She told Kristoff that Anna was going to Brock to get her memories back.

"Bad idea," Kristoff said. "We don't know what Brock is really up to."

"*I* do!" Anna insisted.

203

Kristoff looked at Anna doubtfully. "And how much did you know about Prince Hans before you trusted him?"

Anna scoffed. "That was completely different."

Elsa interrupted. "Kristoff, you lived with the trolls for a long time. Do you know anything about Brock?"

"I don't know him well," Kristoff replied. "He's not like other trolls. He lives outside the troll village in a strange hut. Before he moved out on his own, his attempts at mystical powers always caused accidents. The trolls call him Brock the Rock, because he's about as smart as a rock."

"I saw him during the day!" Anna

offered. "Trolls are usually only seen at night. Maybe that means he really is mystical."

"Or maybe it just means he's strange," Kristoff replied.

"Hmm, maybe he's not the best choice," Elsa said gently. "Could we go to see Grand Pabbie?"

Kristoff shook his head. "Grand Pabbie's hibernating for a while," he said. "He'll be back when the seasons turn."

"I'm not waiting till the seasons turn!" Anna said. "I'm giving Brock a chance!"

"Then it's settled." Elsa gave a nod. "We're going to see Brock, and Kristoff is coming with us. Don't make me *command* it," she added with a smile.

205

Anna smiled, too. As the Queen of Arendelle, Elsa had a way of getting what she wanted. Anna was glad that today, what Elsa wanted was to help her sister, even if it was a long shot. The three friends set off into the forest.

Chapter 7

It was several hours before Anna found the familiar trail through the forest. She, Elsa, and Kristoff followed the path. They crossed the stone bridge over the babbling creek. At last, they came to Brock's grassy hut.

Anna knocked on the round wooden door. The three visitors heard shuffling inside. Moments later, the door flew open. Brock's shaggy head popped out.

"Just Anna! It's you! And you've brought friends!" Brock cried excitedly. He stood back and waved them into his home.

Anna, Elsa, and Kristoff ducked through the small round door. Elsa and Anna sat down beside the fire pit in the center of the hut. Brock sat across from them. There wasn't enough room near the fire for Kristoff. He wedged himself into a corner and sat down on a pile of moldy books.

"No, no!" Brock said. "Do not crush the books! Books are our friends!"

Kristoff frowned. He stood with his head ducked and his shoulders hunched.

Anna introduced everyone to Brock. The troll recognized Elsa. "Brock the Mystical, my queen," he said, and gallantly kissed her hand. He also knew of Kristoff, the man-child raised by trolls.

"Dreadful manners," Brock said, staring at Kristoff.

"I'll say," Anna agreed with a grin. Kristoff smirked at her.

Changing the subject, Anna told Brock that she had come to take him up on his offer. She wanted her memories of Elsa's magic back. Now that everyone knew about Elsa's powers, there was no reason for Grand Pabbie's spell to stay in place. It was time for her to remember.

"I was hoping you'd change your mind, my lady," Brock said. He clapped his hands delightedly. He looked confident and eager to get to work.

Maybe this will actually work, Anna thought.

To restore Anna's memories, Brock said, he had to brew a special potion.

Kristoff's frown deepened. "Grand Pabbie never brews potions," he said. The elder troll's powers came from within. Potions had nothing to do with them.

Elsa noticed Kristoff's frown and gave him a warning glance. Kristoff grumbled but said nothing more.

Brock sent his three visitors into the forest to gather special plants. The plants would make up the ingredients for his potion. Elsa, Anna, and Kristoff split up to find the ingredients.

Anna made her way through the woods. She was looking for a plant called Wyrm's Tail. Brock had told her that it grew in dark places, like underneath rocks.

Anna picked up the rocks and stones

along her path. Eventually, she found one with a plant growing under it. The plant had long, spindly branches that looked like worms. She carefully pulled it out of the dark soil, roots and all.

On her way back to Brock's hut, she met Elsa. Elsa carried a handkerchief full of fresh herbs.

"Do you really think this will work, Anna?" Elsa asked.

Anna thought for a moment. "I hope it will," she said. "It's important for me to have my memories, Elsa. *All* of my memories."

"Then I hope it works, too," Elsa said.

Back at Brock's hut, a fire blazed under a bubbling cauldron. The ingredients had all

been gathered. Brock tossed them into the pot. He stirred them together. The little troll beamed happily as his potion brewed.

Steam rose from the cauldron. Anna, Elsa, and Kristoff wrinkled their noses. The smell was awful.

"How do you think the potion works?" Anna whispered to Elsa.

"I'm not sure," Elsa answered. "But I have a feeling you'll have to drink it."

"All of these herbs are safe to eat," Kristoff chimed in. "But I wouldn't want to taste it."

Ten minutes later, the potion was ready. Anna's worst fears were confirmed. Brock dipped a cup into the smelly brown brew. He handed it to Anna.

"Drink, my lady," Brock said. "It's a memory draught. It will help restore your past."

Anna pinched her nose with her fingers. She closed her eyes and quickly gulped the potion down.

"Yuck!" she exclaimed.

"Splendid!" Brock said. He circled the cauldron three times on his stocky legs. All the while, he chanted in a mysterious language. Brock said that it was the secret language of the trolls.

"I didn't know the trolls had a secret language," Anna whispered.

"They don't!" Kristoff scoffed from his place in the corner.

"Silence, Book Crusher!" Brock said.

Kristoff clamped his mouth shut. He folded his arms across his chest and rolled his eyes.

Brock turned his attention back to Anna. He explained that she, too, would have to circle the cauldron. Anna stood and started to walk, but Brock interrupted her.

"Ah, I should have been more specific," he said. "You'll have to hop around the pot on one foot."

Anna hopped awkwardly around the cauldron. Kristoff grinned at her from the corner. She knew she must look absolutely ridiculous. Anna scowled at Kristoff, but she kept hopping.

"Very good," Brock said when Anna

was done. "Now cluck like a chicken."

Anna exchanged a doubtful glance with her sister. Was Brock serious?

Elsa shrugged. "Sometimes there's no explaining magic," she whispered.

Reluctantly, Anna clucked. She clucked for at least five minutes. Finally, Brock told her it was okay to stop. When she did, the hut was silent, except for Kristoff snickering in the background.

Anna glared at him, but she didn't have time to stay angry.

"The magic is complete!" Brock announced. "It's time to test your memories, Just Anna."

Chapter 8

Anna looked at Brock, puzzled. She didn't feel much different than she had a few minutes earlier. Her stomach was queasy from the awful potion, but she didn't think that was because of magic. It seemed impossible that hopping and clucking could bring her memories back.

Anna thought about the way Elsa's magic worked. She didn't have to hop about or make strange noises. It wasn't silly. If anything, it was beautiful. Elsa could make snow appear. She could build castles of ice with a twirl of her fingers. She didn't need a cauldron.

But Anna was still hopeful. Just because Brock's magic looked different didn't mean it didn't work.

"Now I'm going to ask you some questions, Just Anna," Brock said. "The answers will prove that my magic has worked!"

Anna nodded. Elsa looked at Brock expectantly.

"First question: what color is the sky?" Brock asked.

"Blue," Anna answered.

The troll looked very pleased. "What color is your hair?" he asked.

"Red," Anna replied easily.

"What does this have to do with anything?" Kristoff grumbled.

"I beg you not to interrupt, Book Crusher," Brock said. Kristoff opened his mouth to argue, but Elsa silenced him with a look.

Brock looked eagerly at Anna. "What is your favorite food?"

"Chocolate," Anna said.

"Aha!" Brock exclaimed. "Success! Your memory is saved, Just Anna!"

"Brock, you offered to restore my memories of Elsa's magic! From our

childhood! None of those questions had anything to do with magic!" Anna said.

Brock the Mystical scratched his chin thoughtfully. "Oh, right," he said. "I knew I forgot something. Maybe you should cluck some more."

Anna's mind clouded with disappointment. Brock wasn't mystical. He certainly wasn't going to be powerful like Grand Pabbie. He was nothing more than a kooky little troll who liked to brew awful potions.

Anna's shoulders slumped. She glanced at Elsa and Kristoff, expecting them to say "I told you so." But they both looked just as disappointed as she felt. Anna realized suddenly that they both had been hoping it would work, too. They really cared about her. It made Anna feel just a little bit better.

"Listen, Anna, maybe you should try to remember something about *us*," Elsa said quietly.

"Like what?" Anna asked sadly.

"Like anything," Elsa replied. "Like that time we went ice fishing by ourselves on the frozen lake."

Anna's face brightened. She remembered that story like it was yesterday. Eagerly, she shared it with Kristoff, Brock, and Elsa.

Elsa and Anna's mother, the Queen of Arendelle, used to take her daughters ice fishing. The queen had loved to fish with her family since she was a little girl. She was good at it, too. She was proud to pass on the tradition to her daughters.

In the winter, the queen would take the princesses to the frozen lake. She taught them how to build a shelter on the ice. Once inside the shelter, the queen carved a hole in the ice. She showed Elsa and Anna how to bait their hooks and cast their fishing lines. They would sit all day with their

lines lowered through the hole. They kept warm in their shelter, waiting for the fish to bite.

One day, the girls asked their father to take them ice fishing. The queen was away visiting relatives. He promised to take Elsa and Anna the next day, but the sisters just couldn't wait.

Eight-year-old Elsa and five-year-old Anna grabbed their fishing lines. They bundled up in their warmest coats. When no one was looking, they sneaked out of the castle.

Back in the present, Kristoff interrupted Anna's story with a question. "You two made it all the way from the castle to the frozen lake by yourselves?" he asked.

Anna considered his question. Her brow furrowed in thought. "I guess we did," she said uncertainly. The more she thought about it, all she could remember was snow and laughter.

"Actually, we didn't. We had help," Elsa said.

Anna noticed the glimmer of mischief in her sister's eyes. "You used your powers," she said.

Elsa nodded. She explained that she'd built a magical sailboat out of ice. The

sails were spun from a delicate web of snowflakes. The winter wind blew and filled the snowflake sails, carrying the sisters all the way to the frozen lake.

Anna shared more of the story. Once they'd arrived at the lake, they built a shelter, just like their mother had taught them.

"Well, not *just like* she taught us," Elsa said.

Anna glanced at her sister again. Elsa admitted that she'd used her powers then, too. She'd built them a miniature castle on the ice.

Anna remembered that they'd stayed out all afternoon and caught a lot of fish.

Elsa chimed in to add the magical details. The ice boat had carried them home with their baskets of fish. Elsa froze the fish and snuck them into the kitchens.

"Fishsicles!" five-year-old Anna had shouted in delight.

Afterward, the royal family had eaten fish for weeks. The king and queen never knew exactly why there was so much fish at the dinner table.

"This is wonderful!" Brock said when the story was over. "My magic saved the day!" Before they could pull away, the troll spread his arms wide and squeezed Anna, Elsa, and Kristoff together in an awkward hug. Unfortunately, he accidentally kicked

a burning coal from beneath the pot.

The coal leaped across the room. It landed next to the pile of moldy books in the corner. Seconds later, one of the books caught fire!

"What's that smell?" Anna asked.

Kristoff broke free of Brock's group hug. He spotted the burning book in the corner of the hut. "Fire!" he yelled. Immediately, Kristoff raised his foot to stomp out the flames.

Brock wailed unhappily. "Stop, Book Crusher! Don't crush my books!" The troll dove across the hut and grabbed the flaming book. He juggled it in his hands like a hot potato.

"What are you doing?" Kristoff shouted angrily.

"Saving a friend!" Brock cried. He tossed the book out of the hut, beyond Kristoff's reach.

The book sailed through the air. It landed in a patch of dry bushes and quickly sent them up in flames. Anna, Elsa, Kristoff, and Brock raced outside. What they saw wasn't pretty. The forest was catching fire!

Chapter 9

Brock the Rock looked on in horror. The fire was spreading rapidly. It leaped from bush to bush. Some of the trees were even starting to catch—Anna hadn't noticed until that moment that most of the tall trees around Brock's clearing were dead and dry, their brown leaves dangling from their branches. The orange flames crackled and hissed.

Burning leaves tumbled from the trees. The leaves landed on the roof of Brock's grass cottage. Within seconds, the roof caught fire.

"Oh, no!" Brock shouted. He waved his arms frantically. The kooky troll had no idea what to do. He puckered his lips and blew at the flames, hoping to put them out.

"Stop!" Kristoff cried. "This is a forest fire, not a birthday cake! You can't just blow it out!"

Kristoff leaped into action. He heaved his shoulder against the side of the burning grass hut. Anna saw what he was trying to do. She and Elsa pushed against

the sides of Brock's house and knocked it to the ground.

Once the flimsy grass house had fallen, Anna, Elsa, and Kristoff stomped out the flames.

"I'm sorry, Brock," Anna said.

Anna heard a branch crack and looked up at the trees surrounding the clearing. The flames were spreading even farther than she'd thought. She saw her sister gazing at the fire and caught her eye. She could tell Elsa was about to use her magic. She gave her a questioning look.

"It's too big," Elsa said. "I'm not sure I can do it alone."

Brock looked sadly at what was left of

his home. Elsa placed a gentle hand on his shoulder. "We'll build you a new house, Brock, I promise. But right now we have to stop this fire!"

"That's right," Anna said to the troll. "Just think, what would Grand Pabbie do?"

At the mention of Grand Pabbie, Brock's face brightened. "Grand Pabbie would help put out the fire!"

"We need buckets!" Kristoff called, watching the flames. "Anything we can use to carry water."

"I have an idea, Just Anna!" Brock said.

He poked through the smoldering grass of his house. After a moment, he pulled out the large cauldron, along with

several cooking pots. "Will these do?" he asked.

"Brock, they're perfect!" Anna said. She picked up the cauldron and handed the pots to Kristoff. Brock found some old buckets and raced to the nearby brook.

Anna, Kristoff, and Brock filled their pots with water while Elsa sprayed the trees with ice. Anna paused to watch her sister. It seemed that for every tree she put out, two more caught fire.

The others lugged the water back to Brock's house and tossed it on the burning trees. The fire kept spreading. The flames were growing higher and higher.

Kristoff realized that they couldn't

carry enough water to put out the flames. "We need help!" he said.

Anna volunteered to run to the valley and gather more trolls to help fight the fire. She hurried through the forest to where she remembered meeting the trolls before. Anna rounded up as many as she could. They were eager to help. They followed Anna through the woods.

By the time Anna returned, the clearing where Brock's house had been was engulfed in flames. Elsa, Kristoff, and Brock had fallen back deeper into the forest.

Anna organized the volunteers. She had them form a chain from the brook to the clearing. She stood in the stream, filling

pots with water. They passed the pots down the line of trolls. At the opposite end of the line, Kristoff and Brock were waiting. They tossed pot after pot of water on the fire.

The fire sizzled and hissed. Smoke rose high into the air. Finally, the flames in the clearing began to die down. But by then it was too late. The fire had spread too far. Flames darted across the treetops. A cloud of thick smoke hung over the woods.

Elsa was trying to control the spreading by putting out the fire one tree at a time. "This isn't working fast enough!" Anna heard her sister call out. "I need to see which way it's going!"

Just then, Anna saw something large rising out of the forest. Elsa was using her magic to form a tall column of ice under her feet. Now she would be able to see the entire fire. Elsa raised her arms toward the sky and closed her eyes, deep in concentration.

A cold wind began to blow. It rustled through the leaves. The trolls stopped passing pots. They looked at Elsa.

Elsa opened her eyes. She weaved her hands through the air. A thick blanket of snow drifted down from the clouds above the forest.

The snow fell heavily onto the flames. The fire hissed and sputtered, but it was

no match for Elsa's powers. The magical snowflakes simply outnumbered the embers. Soon the sparks were smothered. The flames had died out at last.

Chapter 10

After the smoke cleared, the trolls gave a hearty cheer. They were relieved that Queen Elsa had stopped the fire and that no one had been hurt. The forest was safe once again.

The trolls invited Brock to stay with them until his hut was rebuilt. Anna, Elsa, and Kristoff helped him gather his belongings from the rubble. The damage wasn't as bad as they had first thought. They were even able to save some of his moldy books.

Brock was still convinced that his potion had restored Anna's memories. Kristoff was eager to tell him the truth, but Anna didn't have the heart. Brock had tried his best to help her. The troll deserved to remember as much magic as he wanted to.

That night at the castle, Anna and Elsa sat down to dinner. Anna was excited to recall the day's events.

"I can't believe I actually clucked like a chicken!" she said.

"I can't believe you actually drank that

awful potion," Elsa laughed. "The smell was horrible!"

Anna thought about how determined she had been to get her memories back. It had been important to her to remember on her own. Only that morning, she had felt like a puzzle with pieces missing. But this afternoon, all that had changed.

Anna realized that her memories weren't missing. As long as Elsa was there, the puzzle was complete. Elsa could remember the magic and Anna could remember the laughter. Together, they were a winning combination.

Elsa looked at Anna across the

dinner table. She must have noticed the thoughtful expression on her sister's face. "I'm sorry I didn't tell you sooner about your memories, Anna," she said. "But I'll always be here for you. We can help each other remember."

Anna nodded. She got up from the table, walked over to Elsa, and hugged

her sister tight. "I have just one question for you," she said. "How come I can't remember all the times we built snowmen together?"

Anna still found that very strange. She had only bits and pieces of those memories. She remembered finding buttons to use for eyes. She remembered sneaking carrots from the kitchens to use as noses. She even remembered gathering hats and scarves for the snowmen to wear. But she could never remember building an actual snowman with Elsa.

"Snowmen were your favorite, Anna," Elsa said. "You were always asking me to make them."

Anna always said that her sister built the best snowmen. Elsa knew how to make special snowman snow—fluffy enough to carry but wet enough to pack into the perfect snowball. Elsa's snowmen always seemed so real. It was easy to imagine their button eyes winking in the light and their carrot noses twitching in the crisp winter air.

On the morning of Anna's fifth birthday, she woke up to a soft sprinkle of snowflakes above her bed. They drifted down from the ceiling of her room. But these weren't

just any snowflakes. Each one was like a tiny sculpture made of ice crystals. One snowflake looked just like Anna! Another looked like Elsa! There were reindeer snowflakes and snowflakes of the king and queen. Best of all, there were snowman snowflakes!

Anna was delighted. She noticed that the snowflakes were falling in a clear path leading out of her room. Eagerly, she hopped out of bed and followed the snowflake path through the castle.

The path led downstairs and out the front door. Anna pulled on a warm coat and followed the trail outside to the royal sleigh.

In the sleigh, Elsa was waiting.

"Happy birthday, Anna!" she told her sister.

Anna giggled happily.

A team of reindeer pulled the sleigh. They drove the sisters all the way to the frozen fjord. There, Elsa gave Anna her birthday present. It was a brand-new pair of ice skates!

Elsa helped Anna lace up her skates. The sisters stepped out onto the fjord. They glided easily across the ice.

Anna and Elsa skated together all afternoon. They whirled and twirled and carved pictures into the ice. Elsa even carved a beautiful picture of Anna wearing a birthday crown.

As evening fell, the girls stopped skating. It was time to build a special snowman for Anna's birthday. Elsa swirled her fingers through the air. She created a mound of her famous snowman snow.

Together, Anna and Elsa rolled the snow into three giant snowballs. Elsa stacked them on top of each other. Anna was excited. She wanted to stick on the button eyes and carrot nose, but she was too short. Elsa created a small set of ice steps for her sister. Anna climbed the steps and made the snowman's face.

That night, Elsa led a sleepy Anna to bed. She tucked her little sister in and said good night. Anna drifted off to sleep.

The next morning, Anna ran to Elsa's bedroom and shared her dream. In it, she'd sung and danced with an enchanted snowman. She asked Elsa if she could use her powers to make their snowman dance. Elsa smiled. She told Anna that she couldn't make a dancing snowman, but they could always pretend. Together, they could imagine anything.

Back in the present, Elsa finished sharing the memory. Anna felt another piece of her past slide into place. Hearing Elsa tell

the story was almost like being there.

"It's funny, Elsa," Anna said. "I was so worried about not being able to remember your magic, I forgot about the magic right here."

"What do you mean?" Elsa asked.

"This. Us," Anna replied. "There's magic in remembering together."

"There sure is," Elsa said. She smiled.

She and Anna walked out of the dining room. They'd had a long day fighting a forest fire and remembering the past. Soon it would be time to go to bed. As they walked up the grand staircase to their rooms, Anna turned to her sister.

"You know, Elsa, snowmen aren't my favorite anymore," she said.

"Really?" Elsa asked. "You seem pretty fond of Olaf."

"Oh, yes, I love Olaf, but he's not my favorite," Anna replied. "You are."

© Jenn Carvin Photography

Erica David has written more than forty books and comics for young readers, including Marvel Adventures *Spider-Man: The Sinister Six.* She graduated from Princeton University and is an MFA candidate at the Writer's Foundry in Brooklyn. She has always had an interest in all things magical, fantastic, and frozen, which has led her to work for Nickelodeon, Marvel, and an ice cream parlor, respectively. She resides sometimes in Philadelphia and sometimes in New York, with a canine familiar named Skylar.